QUEEN of the WORLD WALKERS

JO STEWART WRAY

INK START MEDIA
5710 W Gate City Blvd Ste K #284
Greensboro, NC 27407

*I would like to thank my husband Richard, my family,
Patsy Boyles McElroy, and Judy Collins Graham
for their support.*

Chapter 1

Mother's Day 2021 is turning out to be a good day. Although a slight breeze is blowing from the north, the weather is sunny and bright. The day is beautiful. We haven't had many beautiful days this spring. The meteorologist on WABG television Channel 7 says that there is no cloud coverage. She always talks about cloud coverage like it is the most important thing to say about the weather -not tornadoes, not hurricanes, not rain, just no cloud coverage or lots of cloud coverage whichever the case may be. There isn't a cloud in the sky today, but there are dark clouds on the horizon of my life. As my granny would say, I feel it in my bones. I sit here thinking of my only child Audrey as a toddler and the mess she made the first time she ate pizza by herself. She was sitting in her high chair and although she had a bib, she had tomato sauce all-over her face when the slice was finished or demolished.

Today after eating Italian pizza with lots of cheese and Italian sausage for lunch at the Bistro in Memphis on Beale Street with Audrey, she helps me fill out the ancestry DNA form, her gift to me for Mother's Day. Audrey has done her ancestry research on Google and Yahoo, and even at our local library into our heritage and found ancestors a few hundred years ago all the way to England, but now we want to know more such as who they were and what they did for a living.

Well, she does. For myself, I just want her to be happy. I have spent lots of my life doing something to make her happy. So we have some ancestors from England, I knew that I've always loved Shakespeare. Maybe that is why.

Well, at least, she wants to know about her heritage. She wants to know all the ethnic origins making her who she is. The DNA ancestry form turns out to be more than a pie chart or a bar graph. As far as my DNA goes, I really don't care. It is what it is. For Audrey, it is the adventure of a lifetime. I hope she won't be disappointed by finding all the skeletons in our ancestor's closets and mostly in mine. Anyone my age should have a few skeletons if they've lived at all. I had heard my grandmother mention a few of these skeletons. Although these she talked about were my grandfather and her siblings like my grandfather's brother robbed the Bank of New Orleans. There were a few murders and swapping of wives. Perhaps these wouldn't be exposed. I had wanted to know more about these stories, but now I really don't know why I care except that my grandmother wasn't around any more to tell the stories.

"Some of the ancestry timelines go back to fifty generations," Audrey says, her blue eyes shining and her voice high pitched because she is excited. I love to see the shine in her eyes. She picks up the form. "This one will tell when and where your ancestors are from. Oh, Mom. I so hope you like your present. I know you think it is for me. Maybe in part it is. It will tell you all the different ethnicities and people in your DNA. You know, you will have a picture of your family history, and also over five hundred thousand genetic markers. These markers have a bearing on your health and personality. Besides giving you genetics, it will tell anthropology, and history - combined."

Audrey is more exited than I am, but I try to look interested and act excited. I am having a hard time convincing her that I even care about this ancestry analysis, but I really am enjoying the gleam in her eyes. To me, it is more a present for her. That is often the way with presents anyway. I've sometimes bought people things that I wanted for myself like that sweater I bought my sister that I really wanted for myself. I thought she might let me borrow it to wear after she had gotten the new off it. I can't concentrate on filling out a piece of paper; my mind is on my upcoming vacation to England. I'm more interested in real live people, and to say that I'm excited is an understatement. I'm over-the-moon excited about flying to England. I have my itinerary all planned.

"Oh. Thank you," I reply, trying to sound thrilled. "I love you. Are you certain you won't travel with me to England in a few weeks? We would have a blast. Personally, I can't wait to do the Harry Potter Tour and visit Stonehenge, Windsor Castle, and Bath. I still have time to get your tickets on my frequent flyer plan."

"When is your departure date? I know that I probably can't go. You know I have finals and a boyfriend. Remember that I'm graduating from UAB with a degree in business."

"The first of June. Won't you be finished by then?" I ask. "By the way, I am so proud of you. You will make an excellent addition to some busienss."

"I should. Open your mouth. I need a saliva sample. I want to get this in the mail in the morning, so it will be back by the time we leave. Maybe you can visit some of the places where your ancestors lived. Oh, Mom, wouldn't that be fun?"

"If you were going with me, it would be more fun," I reply.

Chapter 2

The morning that we are to catch our flight on Delta Airlines to London, the results of the Mother's Day present DNA test arrive in the mail. I still hope that Audrey is going with me, but that she is just late. She is always late. It is a standing joke in our family that Audrey would be late for her own funeral. I open the envelope, but I don't have time to read the entire DNA report, but I do glance at the pie chart or circle graph. It shows that I am 20% English, 20% French, 10% Irish, 25% Native American, and 25 % Danish. How can that be? I'm more savage than civilized with the Native American and Danish heritage. Maybe that accounts for my temper. They say some tendencies are inherited. I wonder which tribe of Native Americans. I cram the envelope into my purse slash backpack and hurry to the airport. Now, I'm interested. But only because I think these results are incorrect, but I don't know how to prove it or disprove it. Just as I am about to board the plane alone, my phone dings a text from Audrey. I hope she is okay. She is often late, but I fear that she isn't coming. I knew that she wouldn't have told me ahead of time. I don't know how we communicated before cell phones.

"I'm so sorry, Mom, but I won't be able to join you. Have a great time! That guy, Matthew Brown, my boyfriend that I told you about, the one that I'm in love with and planning to marry, asked me last night to go with him to meet his parents in Colorado, so I'm going. I'm expecting to get an engagement ring. I'm afraid not to go. I didn't tell you sooner because I didn't want you to try to talk me out of it. I know you want me to graduate first. I am graduating with a 4.0. I love you. P.S. I wish Daddy was interested in taking trips with you, so I could tell him about our DNA results. And I would have done his DNA test, too. With a last name like Lodbrok, he is probably Danish. I guess that makes me Danish too."

I am seated on the plane, waiting for take off when I remember that the DNA results are in my purse. The airport has Covid 19 protocols, so I'm wearing my mask. They checked for my vaccine results before I entered the plane. I pull the Ancestry report out of my purse to read on the flight. I get engrossed in the results. I forget that I'm on an airplane. Suddenly, before I even know what is happening, we are in the air, but there is turbulence. The plane is in distress, but it straightens out as it rises. I become intrigued with the DNA results, imagining living in all the places and times mentioned in the results. I'm especially interested in the Native American and Danish parts. Soon, we are landing in London, and I feel alone instead of excited. My husband, Audrey's father, left me a year ago. I haven't dated anyone else since we separated. I really don't know why I haven't. I didn't feel like Audrey would approve of any of the guys that interested me. There were a few guys who asked me out at the school where I teach and a few tried to contact me on social media, but none of them interest me. I wonder if I'm still in love with John. Maybe I am. It took me a while to fall in love, so ending it quickly didn't happen.

At the airport, I rent a little car, load my luggage into the back, and stick the DNA test results deep into my backpack purse again. I name this little car Bessie. Driving Bessie on the wrong side of the street, feels so wrong to me. I guess I'm a creature of habit or just an American tourist. At least, I'm wearing my seatbelt, but I feel so out of place. Just as I wish I had hailed a taxi, I am hit head on by another driver. Although I'm buckled up, my head cracks the windshield. Before I lose consciousness, I hear sirens and people rushing to my assistance. I hope someone contacts Audrey. My information is inside my purse. I am rushed to the hospital in an ambulance. I hear them pronounce me DOA. *I'm not dead. Or am I? Is this what dead feels like?* I feel like my body is floating above itself. I make an effort to feel and move all my limbs, but I can't feel my toes on my left foot. I wait for the events of my life to flash before my eyes like I've heard they do. Nothing about my past flashes, but I know that I'm not dead. I've never been dead, but I know this isn't it.

Instead, I get flashes of another life, flashes of another world. I get flashes that match my DNA results. Flashes are flashes and this is my history. How can the two be connected? Then everything smoothes out, and I'm floating like I'm on a magic carpet like in the cartoons. I'm floating high in the corner of a room almost touching the ceiling. My body is lying on a table. There is blood on my head. The light in the room is very bright. It hurts my eyes. My head aches. Over to the east, I see my mother and father patiently waiting for me. I see Granny. She is beckoning to me to come toward the light. She walks into the bright light. Then the light dims back to normal or what used to be normal, but there is still a glow in the room. I don't think I will ever be normal again. I am awake. Or am I? Where am I? Oh, I remember. I'm in England, but I need to be in America. I need to see Audrey, but Audrey hasn't even been born yet.

It is 1912. It should be 2021, but I've gone back in time. When I reentered my body, I am in 1912. Wait, this is a mistake. Who can I tell? Who can help me? I need help. Who is in charge of this? How is this even possible? I'm not dead. I'm not in a hospital in England.

I sit at a pub in England with some Irishmen. My toes still feel strange like they did in the wreck. I can't feel anything with the tips of them, but they throb. It is called phantom pain. I've read about it. I'm having phantom pain. This is definitely not a morgue. This is a pub. These people are drinking, laughing, and having a grand time. I drink my ale, waiting for time to load onto the *Titanic* to travel back to New York City. The ale's taste reminds me of my last birthday party when we celebrated my becoming twenty-nine years old. Again. Which biologically could not have happened. I must get back home quickly to Audrey because she is getting married, but I don't know how to get there. The year is wrong. I have no luggage, but I have my purse, a cross-body that someone gave me for my birthday. I thought that I left the cheetah print backpack somewhere. Maybe I didn't. I find my cell phone. I keep texting Audrey, but she never answers. Then I realize that I'm stuck in 1912. Audrey is in 2021. This is a mistake. I wonder if she has been contacted about my accident. I don't know why I'm texting her. She wasn't even born until 2000. I definitely have no cell service here. I have no bars. No one does. There are no bars on my phone. It says, "No Service." Those in the pub are looking at me and my cell phone strangely. Some of them look frightened. They probably think I'm a witch or an alien or afflicted with a deadly disease or have heart or blood issues. The phone could be a medical device or an alien device, but in 1912? Did they even know what aliens were in 1912? I look at my clothing: Levi button front jeans, a Willie Nelson graphic tee, and a generic gray sweatshirt with a hood. This is the uniform of an American tourist. I know that I was in a car accident, but there isn't any blood on my clothes, but my head hurts and my toes tingle. This is definitely a 2021 tourist outfit. I am an American tourist. My blond hair is pulled into a high top knot ponytail, one of my favorite hair styles, like a Viking female warrior. I think it makes me look younger. I remember my DNA results saying I was 25% Danish and 25% Native

American. I smile. I look around. These people are English and Irish, and they aren't dressed like me. American tourist clothes are what I describe my outfit as. None of the other women waiting to load onto the *Titanic* look like me. Sometimes it is good to be different, but I wonder if I'm invisible. All the women are wearing ankle length dresses with tight, fitted waists. I think about how uncomfortable they must be. They are wearing silks and velvets not denim jeans and a cotton graphic tee. They give the impression of being snobbish and rich. The men don't say or even care anything about my clothes, but they are so drunk and happy that what I am wearing doesn't seem to even register with them, but the women notice. I am not invisible. They notice my clothes. They notice me using my cell phone. They notice my hair style or lack of it. They notice that I seem to be disoriented. They notice that I'm not wearing a wedding ring. They aren't friendly. I see the way they look at each other and roll their eyes. I had read that the English were snobbish. Well, here you go. I remember that this is 1912. I don't think they are as snobbish now in 2021, but they could be. We will see.

My ticket to board the *Titanic* lies on the bar. This bar could use a good cleaning, like we had to do in with Lysol in 2020 because of Covid 19, but there is no Covid 19 here. This ship is the first one going back to the United States that I found. I must get back for Audrey's graduation or at least for her wedding. The ticket's destination is right even if the year isn't. One guy next to me notices my ticket and grabs it. "Hey, blokes, this gorgeous lass is boarding the *Titanic*, too," he yells to the his drunk buddies. The room is full of them. The men smile, but the women don't. He smells of soap. These men don't know their fate.

I grab my ticket back from him and shove it into my purse with my DNA ancestry results. I am very confused. "Why don't I have any cell service? What year is it?" I ask the man sitting at the bar next to me.

"Why, 1912, lass. Are you that drunk? Cell service? What is that?"

"No, just confused. I thought it was 2021," I say. I look around at all the Irishmen in this English pub. They are waiting to get on the *Titanic*, too. Then I remember why I am in England. I remember what happened to the *Titanic*. I remember the car accident after I exited the plane. I remember hitting my head. I remember being pronounced dead, but I'm still here, although it isn't 2021. I am not dead, and I need to get back to America. He says it is 1912. I'm sure that I'm not dead. I'm just insane for boarding the *Titanic* because it will sink. I may really die.

These men have no idea that the *Titanic* is doomed. They have no idea that the *Titanic* is going to sink. I do, but I'm desperate.

"They call the *Titanic* unsinkable," one of the Irishmen says, yelling above the noise of the crowd. "Here's to the unsinkable *Titanic*, the world's largest passenger ship." He raises his glass of Irish whiskey and drinks it in one long gulp. He doesn't seem to feel the burn. It must be an acquired taste.

"Why are you toasting the *Titanic*? Don't you know it is going to sink?" I ask.

"No. We are sailing with multimillionaires. Even John Jacob Astor is on this ship. Do you think all those rich folks don't know what they are doing? How do you think that they got to be so rich?"

"But it hits an iceberg on April 15."

"Lass, you are drunk, and you have a ticket too. If it is going to sink, why are you boarding? Just relax. It is unsinkable. They advertise it as unsinkable. Just go with it. I'll hold your hand, so you won't be frightened." He grabs my hand tightly and drags me outside the pub toward the dock and the ship. The air out here smells fishy but cleaner than that inside the pub. I think about Lysol again.

Holding on to my purse tightly, I let him drag me outside. I have no luggage, but he doesn't either. "What is your name?" I ask. "Where is your family?"

"Lass, I'm not married, and I don't have children to speak about. Well, none that I know about. You?"

"Not now. My husband left a while ago. I do have a daughter. I must get back to America to my daughter. Her name is Audrey. She is graduating from college and getting married."

"Well, then. We are going to have a grand time. You don't look old enough to have a daughter getting married. If she's as pretty as you, no wonder she is getting married." Once aboard, we are escorted below deck to the third class section according to our tickets. It is steerage. Steerage was all I could afford in cash. They didn't take credit or debit cards in 1912. I am frightened. The snobbish porters look at us as if we are invisible, but I feel the Irishman holding onto my hand, and I still have the phantom pain in my toes. I may be a ghost and I may be dead, but he isn't because I can feel his hand touching mine. I feel the warmth. I may be dead, but I see the ship's attributes. The *Titanic* is gorgeous. I remember what I read about the *Titanic*. I remember that I'm already supposed to be dead, so I can't drown. "We won't be up there with the multimillionaires, but we are still going to have a wonderful time. Money isn't everything. Besides, they are snobbish."

The upper deck of the *Titanic* is beautiful. Elegant and rich would be a better description. Mahogany wood waxed to a high shine and thick, carpeted, winding stairs, beautiful dining rooms and state rooms, and wide decks are filled with richly dressed people, wearing furs, satins, silks, velvets, and other beautiful dresses with feathers and plumes. Porters push carts with their huge luggage trunks to their rooms. They are so rich that you can smell it. Wealth oozes from their pores. I feel embarrassed to be wearing the uniform of an American tourist - button front, boot-cut Levi jeans, a Willie Nelson tee-shirt, and a gray no-label sweatshirt with a hood. I can't wait to get below deck and away from the disapproving looks of these snobbish rich people. My mother would have said that they don't need to go out in the rain, because they might drown. Although I feel the classism, I hold my head up high. I know that most of them, especially the men, are going to die in four days. I wonder if they would believe me if I told them. I doubt it. They would label me a witch and take me to the ship's authorities. I would get escorted off the ship before it sets sail. Their wealth can not save them, and although I'm taking a huge chance, I need to get back to Audrey in America, and I will try anything to get there.

Once below deck, steerage looks quite different from the upper deck where the wealthy and millionaires are. The walls, stairs, and doors are metal but covered in white, painted paneling. The paint even smells fresh. I figure it contains lead. Although lead paint is the least of our worries. The benches are crowded together. Suddenly, the other Irishmen from the pub crowd around. They smell like little boys who have been playing outside, the pub they just left, and beer. Then sitting next to them are some poorer looking Englishmen. I think about my DNA results. I think about Audrey. I miss my only child, but that is why I'm taking this chance.

"There aren't any lifeboats for us," I say. "There aren't even enough on the upper deck. I counted." And I had watched the movie *Titanic* a few years ago, but I didn't say that.

"Lifeboats? Sure, lass, I saw lots of lifeboats along the upper deck? Stop worrying. You are too pretty to worry."

"They will lock us inside down here. We will drown. Can you swim? Oh, never mind. It won't help. The sea will be freezing cold. No one can live in that water for very long. The rescuers won't reach us in time."

"No worries, lass." He pulls a long, slender knife from his pocket. It reminds me of a butter knife. "I've got that covered. We won't be locked inside. I can get us out. Let's just have fun. This is an experience of a lifetime. Why don't you just have some fun."" Then he unwraps a musical instrument case that is wrapped in his coat. I had not noticed it before. "We will be dancing and having a grand time in a few minutes. So, relax."

"Over half the women and children down here will perish. They drown or die with hyperthermia," I cry.

"Aw, cheer up, lass," he says. "Are you afraid to sail?"

"Find your bunk. Next to mine." I ask this from more fear than anything else. Although I know I won't be because their are thousands of people, I don't want to be alone on this ship. Being alone in a crowd is hard. I don't want to be on this ship at all. I just want to get home to Audrey in America. I know what is going to happen, but how can I explain to anyone else that I am from 2021 not 1912. They already think I'm insane or drunk. I've heard them say so. No, they think I'm dead. After the car accident, they said I was DOA. I can't imagine that being dead feels like this. I don't want to be far away from the key to the door to get to the lifeboats. I read how they are going to load the boats, and I saw it on the movie. According to it, they will be loaded women and children first and by class. I'm counting on finding a gentle soul to let me get into a lifeboat. I know the ship is going to hit that iceberg. It know it does. I can't change history, no matter how hard I try, but I can steal a life jacket or two.

"I can't bunk next to you, lass. We are in private cabins. The men and women are separated. Find your bunk, and I will meet you in the General Room after we claim our bunks. His eyes dance with excitement. We will continue our conversation there. I want to hear more about your theory about this iceberg. A bloke assured me that they watch for icebergs all the time, day and night. But don't be too serious, tonight we will have a grand party in the General Room. Did you see that piano? I've never played one that new and fancy. We are on our way to America. It is so exciting. We'll party until we get there."

"That's what you don't understand. None of you do. All of us aren't going to make it," I whisper under my breath. "That iceberg will sink us on April 15. This ship will sink within two hours of hitting that iceberg." I look around, admiring the white-painted paneling and the salmon pink linoleum of this brand new ship. I could say it smells like a new doll, but it is really the fresh paint. This ship is impressive even down here in steerage. But it still sinks, impressive or not. The *Titanic* sinks from arrogance.

"After you find your bunk, come back to the General Room. Wear your party dress." He looks at me and winks. "You are a doll."

"I don't have any other clothes except this that I have on," I say. I think I had rather be overboard in the ocean in jeans and a sweatshirt anyway. I look for the restroom. I see that the entire third floor has only two baths, and we from steerage aren't allowed to use the gym or the pool. Somehow, that fact doesn't bother me at all. I can't imagine swimming now when I know we will wind up in the frigid ocean later. I freshen up a little by splashing water on my face and combing the wisps into place and head to the General Room to read over my ancestry DNA paperwork more closely. Right now, it is the only thing that gives me any comfort. I find a bench near the piano. There are posters decorating the wall that advertise the White Star Line of ships. I refresh myself with the DNA results: English, Irish, French, Danish, and Native American. The percent Danish intrigues me most. I've always enjoyed watching the television shows about Vikings. Which countries are Danish? I think Denmark, Sweden, and Norway, but those people also settled England, Ireland, Scotland, Wales, Iceland, Greenland, and even North America. I remember reading that Leif Erickson really discovered America before Columbus. I never really thought much about it. Anyway, I think that my results are wrong. Perhaps they switched my results with someone else's at the lab, or perhaps there was a computer glitch. Audrey wanted this DNA test. I didn't really, but whenever I get back to America, I'm going to check into these mistakes.

I read in the newspaper about that runic inscription on a stone that was found in Minnesota. Supposedly, it was left by the Vikings. When and if I get back home, I'm going to do some research on the Vikings and the Danes who lived in Minnesota, too. I wonder if John was a descendant of the Vikings. If these results are correct, I could find relatives there. I might even move to Minnesota. I just want to be back in America. I don't believe the DNA results anyway.

I stuff my DNA results paperwork back into my purse. I sit thinking about those countries where the Vikings may have settled. The room begins filling with happy men and women. The men still smell like the bar where they had partied. Men aren't allowed to smoke in the General Room, but all must go into the smoking room that has a bar and tables nailed to the floor for card playing. I wonder if they are nailed to the floor because the ocean is rough. I wonder if you can feel the roughness of the swells like you feel turbulence on an airplane. A rowdy card game starts up immediately. These men are having a wonderful time. Actually, it is a continuation of the one earlier at the pub. Someone in the General Room begins playing *When Irish Eyes are Smiling* by Donal O'Shaughnessy on the piano. I think of Audrey and her piano lessons. I wonder if she thinks I'm dead. I wonder if she knows about my car accident.

"There's a tear in your eye And I'm wondering why For it never should be there at all With such pow'r in your smile," someone sings. Then the guy that dragged me onto the ship pulls out his fiddle and begins playing the gig. He is very talented. The Irish girls hike their skirts and begin dancing. *We will party for four days.* I think. And then die. I pick up a bottle someone smuggled in here and drink the rest of it. I don't worry too much about germs. I've already been pronounced DOA. I replace the top and stick it into my purse.

Soon a few of us drift into the Dining Saloon. The food smells fabulous. I am starving. To say that the food is to die for is not going too far. We are to choose from rice soup, Irish stew, fresh bread, roast beef and brown gravy, sweet corn, boiled potatoes, plum pudding, sweet sauce and fruit. All this is prepared by a chef or a group of chefs. I'm hungry. All I remember eating previously is pizza with Audrey. This definitely isn't fast food like in America. This food, although it is less expensive than some on the ship, was cooked by an excellent, well-trained chef.

As we eat our dinner, I tell those next to me about the sinking of the *Titanic*. They look at each other and roll their eyes like I'm a witch or a crazy person, so I decide to shut up. If I don't, they will literally think I'm a witch and report me to the ship's authorities. I might get thrown into the ship's jail. When the ship begins to sink, I definitely don't want to be locked inside a room in the lower decks. Again, I think about the movie *Titanic* and Leonardo DiCaprio locked below deck by a handcuff to a pipe. I need to be able to move freely onto the upper deck area. I need to be able to get in a lifeboat or at least get a lifejacket while floating in the ocean.

I need that lock-picking tool that my Irish friend has, so I make my way back to where he sits with a crew of men playing cards. I lean down and whisper something in his ear, distracting him. He still smells of soap, like Ivory. I run my hand into the pocket of his coat while I'm whispering and retrieve that lock-picking tool. I learned this trick when I was in trouble for writing a letter to my boyfriend in the third grade. My teacher took it and hide it in her jacket pocket. I stole it and flushed it down the commode. She never mentioned it again, and I didn't get in trouble.

I may get separated from him, but I won't be separated from the tool. I have to be able to open the door to the stairwell that leads above deck. As soon as I find a way to get back above deck, I'm going to steal a life jacket. At least, I'll have that to help keep me alive after we sink. I might steal more than one. I don't know because I don't want to be greedy. Greed and arrogance are the cause of *Titanic's* sinking anyway.

Tomorrow I'm going to dry the inside of an ale bottle, put a message inside, and replace the cap tightly. When I'm above deck, I'm going to throw the bottle into the Atlantic Ocean. I have always wanted to do that to see what would happen. It might make it all the way to America even if I didn't.

Chapter 3

Early the next morning, my chance comes. I am inside the stairwell near the upper deck waiting for my opportunity whenever one of the porters accidentally leaves the door open. I sneak out onto the upper deck with the upper class passengers. Intrigued, I move from shadowy hiding place to shadowy hiding place watching and listening to their conversations. Listening to conversations is a hobby of mine. Some are English, but some are American. I see one woman named Margaret Brown, who recently got very wealthy in mining. I think in Colorado. Her nickname is Molly. The real Margaret Brown is rather attractive. She's more attractive that Kathy Bates who played her in the movie. She has pin curls in her brown hair and a center part. The pin curls remind me of the way my mother and her sister wore their hair whenever they were in high school. She wears tons of lace that reminds me of a Magnolia Pearl specialty dress except it has a fitted waist, and isn't oversized. Magnolia Pearl is lagenlook. Well, that is what I saw on the movie about the *Titanic* about Mrs. Margaret Brown. The English women whisper about her calling her "new money." Frankly, to me, money is money, and currently, I have none, and nobody here takes plastic. I don't think I'd mind being called "new money." Wealth is wealth.

I think about what I've read about Molly Brown. She is called "The Unsinkable Molly Brown" after the *Titanic* sinks and she survives. Perhaps, I can stick close to her because she is one of the survivors. I decide to introduce myself to her. I decide to befriend her.

What can it hurt? After all, I am an American from 2021, and she is American from 1912. We don't believe is classes or racism. It isn't politically correct. Right?

I see my chance. Like on the movie, the snobbish English women have contrived an excuse to leave Margaret Brown sitting alone, so she is sitting and reading in the sun by herself. Perhaps sitting alone is her choice. From watching the *Titanic* movies, I remember the other old money rich ladies shun her behind her back. I hope it is true that they shun her because I figure she will talk to me and possibly help me later because I befriended her. From my vantage point in the shadows, she looks to be friendly.

I sit in a vacant lounge chair next to Mrs. Brown and strike up a conversation. She smells of roses. The air is brisk and I think about the iceberg, but the sun feels marvelous on my face. I ask her about her husband and the mining business at the Little Jonny Mine in Colorado. She looks at me with interest because I know details about her and I'm American. I tell her that I know she has been traveling with the John Jacob Astor party. He is probably the richest man on the ship. I tell her that she will go down in history as a heroine.

"How do you know about it?" she asks, looking at me with interest. "Are you psychic?"

"Mrs. Brown? Margaret? If I told you how I know about you, you wouldn't believe me. You would think me a witch. I am not. I will tell you my story if you promise not to call the ship authorities on me."

She smiles. She looks intrigued. "I can always use some entertainment," she says. "A witch? Well, I want to hear this story." We sit there until I have told her everything about myself. I tell her about the ancestry DNA test that Audrey gave me for Mother's Day. I know Mother's Day is in May and this is April, but I'm getting to that. I show her the DNA results on paper. I show her the date on the paper. I tell her this date proves that I am from the future. I tell her about my original trip to England to research my ancestors and to have fun.

"My parents were Irish Catholic immigrants," she says. "How is an ancestry DNA test done? I've never heard of it, but I'd like to have one done."

"With a saliva test," I reply. "DNA testing begins in 1984."

She becomes very quiet. "So I can't have one done? Not for 72 more years. I'm afraid I won't live that long."

"On a lighter note, you will be famous after this voyage, and that lady in Denver that you want to invite you to a bridge game…well…after you become famous, she will be clamoring to get you to join her bridge club."

She looks at me with renewed interest. "How can you know that?"

"Remember, I'm from the future. I read a book about your life."

Then I tell her about my car accident in London. I tell her that I was pronounced dead, but ended up on this ship sailing back to America instead of in a casket being shipped back home for burial. "I need to get back to America as soon as possible. My daughter is getting married."

As I converse with Margaret Brown, I watch what is happening on the deck of the ship. "Your nickname becomes The Unsinkable Molly Brown," I say. I refrain from telling her about the *Titanic* sinking on April 15 at 2:20 A.M., three days from now. I figure she really will think I'm a witch if I give her the exact time. She must take the nickname to mean "a person who rises from adversity" because she doesn't ask how she got that nickname. I sit there long enough to know that some of the life jackets are kept inside the lifeboats, and to my good luck, one of the lifeboats is lowered from the position where it hangs waiting to be needed. Suddenly, the dinner horn sounds. The loud sound startles me. I jump. The crew members are just out of sight around the corner.

"You are an interesting young woman, Heidi. What did you say your last name was?"

"It is Lodbrok. I think it is Danish."

"Of course, I remember from your pie chart. You are a large percent Danish and Native American. In Colorado, we call them Indians. After we get back to the States, look me up, Miss Lodbrok. It would be very helpful to have a friend from the future." Soon Mrs. Brown leaves. I watch her speak to the people on deck as she makes her way to her quarters. Not once did she condescend to me. Not once did she ask me about my clothes. Not once did she indicate that I was on the wrong section of the ship. I am certain that she didn't know what to think about my ancestry DNA report. I don't truly understand how it works myself. At least she was very kind. I sit there until she is out of sight, I sneak across the deck and raise the tarp-like covering and slip one of the life jackets out of the life boat. Quickly, in the shadow of the lifeboat, I remove my sweatshirt. I put on the life jacket hiding all the straps, and put the sweatshirt back on over it. No one will be the wiser. I just look fat or pregnant. I remember that looking pregnant could get me a seat in one of the lifeboats. I make myself a promise to find The Unsinkable Molly Brown if indeed I make it back to America in 1912, or if I do make it back and need a job. I know that she does. I read all about her.

I take the ancestry DNA results from my purse and the White Star Ale bottle that I sneaked from the General Room. I roll the paper into a small enough tube to fit into the neck of the bottle, and then I screw the top on as tightly as I can. I tiptoe to the side of the ship and look at the vast Atlantic Ocean. I think about floating in it later after the ship sinks. Then I drop the bottle overboard. I've memorized the DNA results. Besides, if I make it back to 2021. I'm already dead. Or am I? I feel very alive and afraid to be on the *Titanic*. If you are dead, can you feel afraid. I guess you can because I do.

I rush back to the entrance to the stairwell that returns to steerage. It is locked. I pick the lock by sticking the lock-picking tool in the hole and twisting it ever so gently. I wiggle it slightly. I giggle it. The gate swings open.

Just as I'm slipping through the gate, a voice yells, "Hey? What are you doing?" It is a porter.

I rush down the stairwell as fast as my legs will take me. I leave the gate open. Maybe he will stop to lock it. I rush back to my private bunk area and quickly remove the sweatshirt and the life jacket. I take my ponytail loose. I need to look different, so he won't recognize me. I shove the two pieces under the bunk mattress and rush back to the General Room without my black sweatshirt. Once I'm sitting there listening to the music, that same porter enters the room. I watch him out of the corner of my eye. I never turn to look at him. I try to act as if nothing has happened. He looks around. I'm hoping that he is looking for a black sweatshirt on a fat man. He sees no one fitting that description, so he leaves.

I let out a long sigh of relief. Maybe tomorrow I will go back above deck to search for Mrs. Margaret Brown. She is very entertaining and very nice, and may be my only way to get out of this situation alive. So far, she is the only person I've talked to on this ship except the Irishmen from the pub, but I didn't care to talk to the snobbish English women, the ones that on the movie snub Molly Brown.

A young mother with two toddlers comes to sit on the bench next to me. She is very beautiful in a natural sort of way. Her skin is creamy and dark curls frame her face. Her children look like she probably looked as a child with curly dark hair and big brown eyes. They are beautiful. "I'm so sad," she says. "I dreamed that this ship sinks and we all drown." She has tears in her eyes.

I want to say, "Not all of us." But I don't know who survives and who doesn't, so I just smile sadly at her. I hope she doesn't notice my sadness. When it is time, I will get her a life jacket, too. I will try to help her.

"Why do you dress in men's clothing? It is clear to see that you are a beautiful woman," she asks in broken English. I think that her native language is French. French women haven't been wearing pants yet except those who work in the fields.

I look down at my tee shirt and jeans. There is no way I'm going to try to explain being from the future to her, especially since I just threw the ancestry DNA results overboard. She probably can't read English anyway.

"I'm sorry. I must go to the restroom," I say.

"Restroom?" she asks.

"Bath," I say.

"Ah," she nods.

Chapter 4

The next two days, I sneak back onto the upper deck to find Molly Brown. I remember that this is possibly the last time I will see the sunshine and feel its warmth on my skin. I feel so cold down below deck. I don't wear the black sweatshirt and I wear my hair in a tight braid this time so that if that porter is around, he won't recognize me. Hoping to see her, I walk to the same location on the deck where I met Margaret Brown before. There she sits reading in the sun. She is reading *The Secret Garden* by Frances Hodgson. When I get back to America, I make a mental note to read it.

"Hello, Mrs. Brown," I say. "This sunshine feels so good."

She looks up from her book. "Hello, Mrs. Lodbrok. How are you doing today?"

"Fine," I reply. "It is a pretty day. Isn't it?"

"Yes," she replies. "I see that you aren't wearing your jacket today. I want you to do something for me. I brought you something." She motions to the brown paper wrapped package lying in the seat next to her. "Sit and talk with me. My daughter was supposed to make this voyage with me, but she is studying in Europe. She had packed these clothes in my luggage before she decided not to travel with me. I'm giving them to you. You look to be her size."

"Thank you, Mrs. Brown. You are so kind." Although I was surprised, I didn't want to refuse the gift and be rude. I figured my waist was way too large for these fashions.

"You will fit in better here dressed like a woman. Although the women, won't treat you any better. Probably worse. Hmmm? You are an attractive woman. They don't have your American confidence. Confidence is very attractive, so I've been told."

"I've only spoken to two women on this ship. You were one of them,"

I reply. "The other barely spoke any English. She was a French woman with two small children."

"Women are sometimes cruel. Aren't they?" She motioned for me to open the package. "Aren't there parties below deck? Otherwise, when we reach New York, you will want to fit in. I know you explained that you are from 2021, but no one there will know that or believe you. It will be better if you blend in."

"Thank you," I say. "You are so kind, Mrs. Brown. I'm glad I had the opportunity to meet you. I extend my hand. I'm not very good at blending in."

"I've decided to hire you to be my secretary whenever we reach New York. I do some philanthropic work, and a young lady who knows what is happening in the future surely would be an asset. It is a good thing you arrived here and didn't arrive in Salem, Massachusetts, or you would be burned at the stake for being a witch." She laughs at her own joke. "What was your job before?"

"I was a high school teacher back in America. Again, thank you. I really don't know what to say. I don't tell her that the witches weren't burned at the stake. They were hung or drowned, but either way they died. Writers made the burned at the stake thing famous. I'm glad I didn't arrive in Salem too, but I desperately want to get back to America. I had a job when I left America, but that was in 2021. I was a high school history teacher. At one school, I taught English literature, too."

"I would like to invite you to dinner tonight in the States Room. The food on board this ship is fabulous. Would you like to come? I'd like to show you off as my American assistant." She had that huge grin plastered across her face. "Oh, please do. Now, you don't have an excuse because you have something to wear. You will look beautiful."

"Will the ship's authorities throw me overboard if they see me in the wrong section?" Once again, I'm thinking about the *Titanic* movie.

"Not wearing that outfit and sitting with me at the Captain's table." She nods toward the large brown package lying next to her. A huge, stupid smile again spreads across her face. I feel like she is trying to show up the old money crew, so I think it will be fun. She reaches across and touches my cheek. Her touch is warm. "I like to irritate people just a little." She winks at me. "I hope you don't mind. I can't wait to see the expressions of their rich faces."

"You can spend the rest of this afternoon getting ready for dinner tonight with the Captain, Captain Smith. Oh, and if I were you, I wouldn't tell the women left at the table after the men leave to smoke and drink brandy that you are from the future. Actually, if I were you, I wouldn't mention it to anyone. Their pointed teeth might come out like vampires." She cackles with laughter. Thinking of their pointed teeth smiles must give her huge satisfaction. Her laugh is infectious, so I smile too. I don't think I've smiled since I boarded this ship or had the car accident.

I decide that she is a woman before her time. Her personality would definitely fit in 2021 where Americans are more relaxed and less prim and proper. She isn't reserved at all. And from her success, I know that she is smart. Very smart.

"I bought a ticket on this voyage because my grandson has become very ill," she says. "I need to get back to America."

"I am so sorry. I hope he gets better," I reply. "I need to get back to America too."

"Since you know things, I don't suppose you happen to know how his illness turns out," she asks.

I shake my head, no. Finally, I take the package of clothes that she has given me. I thank her again and head back to the stairs and below deck. No one is guarding the entrance, so I slip the lock-picking tool into the key hole, and it clicks open. I leave it open this time too. Leaving it open may be a dangerous thing to do. So I pull it closed, but it doesn't lock like a motel room. The key must be inserted to relock it.

Excited as a child at Christmas, I hurry back down the stairs to steerage and rush into the bathroom to open my brown paper wrapped package. Mrs. Brown has given me a blue silk suit with a columnar skirt and tight fitting bodice that belonged to her daughter. It is dark navy blue silk with pearl and silver buttons. It feels scrumptious touching my skin. The waist is tiny. I wish for a corset or even some Duct tape to cinch my waist like Audrey's cousins use in pageants to hold their waist in and uplift their boobs without a bra that shows in a strapless dress. Then I remember this in 1912, and Duct tape hasn't been invented yet. I didn't want to wear Duct tape anyway. I imagine it is terribly uncomfortable, especially when it gets ripped off. I can't imagine trying to swim while wearing Duct tape. She even included the shoes and undergarments. I don't know how I feel about wearing someone else's undergarments, but since I only have the panties that I have been wearing, I decide that it may be okay. Besides, I have already been pronounced dead. What can her panties hurt? I'm sure that they are clean. The shoes are high top leather boots that lace up. I'm sure it will take a while to put them on and remove them because of all the laces. I also know that my tennis shoes would look funny with the silk skirt. I smile at the thought. I imagine the looks on the rich ladies faces if I came in wearing tennis shoes with this silk dress.

I look in the mirror. My hair is a mess, but I will shampoo it and comb it into an acceptable style. Perhaps I'll ask the French lady with the two toddlers for help. She probably will be able to braid it or something, but I have no pins or barrettes.

I look up and she is entering the bath. Just my luck.

"Oh, you have a package?" She says in her broken English.

"Yes, it was given to me by Mrs. Brown from America. I'm going to dinner with her tonight. And with the Captain." I smile a large smile, showing my teeth.

"Oh, my, my," she exclaims. "The Captain of this ship?"

"Yes. Captain Smith. I was wondering if you could help me do my hair. I was just thinking of shampooing it now, but I don't have any shampoo."

"Oh, yes, Madame. It will be fun to have something to do. I will fetch some French shampoo and hair products, but how will we dry it?"

"I will squeeze most of the water out and use the blanket on my bunk as a towel. That should suck all the water out. I will watch your children while you go to get the hair products."

She says something to them and hurries out the door.

I play with her two toddlers, a boy and a girl that seem to be about a year apart, and soon she returns with her French shampoo. It smells like gardenias. I wish that I had some money to pay her. I decide to give her the clothes and shoes that Mrs. Brown had given me when I get back tonight, because whenever this ship sinks, I want to be wearing my jeans and sweatshirt.

I shampoo my hair and squeeze my hands down the length of it for about ten times until the excess water flows down the drain. Then I towel it dry with the blanket off my bunk until most of it is dry. It smells faintly of gardenias. With my head upside down, I run my hands through my hair to give it volume and detangle it. Some of my natural curls have shown up. I love the gardenia smell of the French shampoo.

The French woman uses rag strips and tight braids to add more curls and waves. "I will give you this dress and shoes after tonight, if you want them. I won't have any need of anything this fancy, and you might." I tell her.

"Oh, no." She insists. "You stay in here. I will come find you whenever it is time to finish your hair. We'll do it half up and half down. Maybe I can find some hairpins."

Finally, it is time for the dinner party. I am excited. I am shampooed, bathed, and my hair is styled in a gorgeous French style with tendrils around my face. I smell wonderful. I think I look nice. I think of my French ancestors and wonder if they dressed this way. I dress in the blue silk outfit and shoes that Mrs. Brown gave me. All are too snug. I'm sure that corsets help keep your waist smaller. There is no room to grow as my grandmother used to say. There is no room to eat a lot either. I open the gate with the lock-picking tool and sneak above deck and head to the States Room. I am fashionably late, but my place at the table next to Mrs. Brown and the Captain Smith is empty. I walk in and drop my chin to my chest saying, "I beg your pardon. I am so sorry to be late."

"Have a seat," Mrs. Brown says, smiling broadly. Captain Smith rises and pulls out my chair and I sit. "I'm so glad to see you. You look lovely."

"My, what a beautiful guest," he says. "Ah, gardenias. My favorite flower. You smell wonderful. You were worth waiting for. You are a refreshing vision of beauty, and you smell wonderful," he repeated.

"Thank you," I reply. I think he is coming on to me. No, I know he is.

"This is Heidi Lodbrok, my secretary," Mrs. Brown introduces me to the others at the table.

"Lodbrok?" Captain Smith asks. "I don't remember that name being on our first class guest list. Lodbrok is Danish. I would remember. It is an unusual name."

"My name is Danish, Captain." I don't give him time to condescend. "Lodbrok is my maiden name. I am American."

"Miss Lodbrok is married to my husband's nephew," Mrs. Brown says, dismissing the question. Then she turns to the others and asks, "Are you enjoying your voyage so far?" She acts as if his question is inconsequential. She acts as if he wouldn't have noticed the name Brown. She is great at controlling the conversation.

Captain Smith is very interested in their answer about their voyage, so he forgets to inquire further about my last name. The first course of our dinner is served before he has a chance to ask me my married name. It tastes wonderful, and I realize that I haven't eaten since breakfast. I am starving. John Lodbrok used to pick at me all the time because he said I was always hungry. I decide to tell Captain Smith that my name is Brown if it will stop the questions. After all Mrs. Brown has said that I'm married to her husband's nephew.

We have up to thirteen courses and each course has a different accompanying wine. We have *pate' de foie gras*, peaches in chartreuse jelly, and Waldorf pudding. I look carefully at my eating utensils. At least, I know to use them in order, but that is about all I know about them. One of them looks exactly like the lock-picking knife that I use to open the door to the stairwell. I am amazed at my luck. Whenever, I don't think anyone if looking, I slip it from the table to my lap and up the sleeve of Mrs. Brown's daughter's dress. I don't figure she ever had to pick a lock, but it looks exactly like the lock-picking tool belonging to the Irishman from the pub. It might come in handy later, and I can return his so he can get above deck too.

By the time dinner is over, I have had way too much wine since we had a different wine with each course. Then the Captain asks if I would like to see the view of the Atlantic Ocean at night from his cabin. He is careful to whisper so that the others don't hear him, but I think Mrs. Brown reads the look on his face. She winks at me and nods. Then she whispers to me not to tell him about being from the future. She says that he would be offended. After all that wine, I knew that I would have to tell him about the ship sinking because I've had too much. What is that they say, 'Loose lips sink ships?' This time it is going to be an iceberg. I also knew that I could not change history no matter what I told him, so I decided to play it by ear as to whether I tell him or not. One thing was for certain, there would definitely be no pillow talk, even if he had to toss me overboard from the deck.

After dinner, Captain Smith and the men leave to smoke and drink brandy, but before he leaves, he leans down and whispers in my ear that he will return quickly to show me his living quarters and the wheel room. They he winks at me and leaves with the men.

As soon as the men are gone, one of the women asks me, "Miss Lodbrok, are you from Colorado as well?"

"Yes." I answer simply without adding anything else. I have never even been to Colorado. Then I turn toward Mrs. Brown and wink.

Mrs. Brown smiles and takes over the conversation about some of her adventures in Europe. She knows I don't want to be quizzed about anything, and she doesn't want them to know that I'm from 2021, so she starts another conversational topic that isn't about me.

Finally, Captain Smith returns, smelling of cigar smoke, and Mrs. Brown and I rise to leave. She escorts me from the room and out the door, but leaves us to go to her own quarters. She gives me a knowing wink. To me the wink says, "Please don't tell him."

I nod my head in agreement. I definitely do not want to alienate her. She could very well be in charge of my survival as the lifeboats are loading.

We make our way toward his living quarters. "Captain Smith, how many lifeboats are on this ship?" I ask.

"I am certain that we are following the rules, Miss Lodbrok," he replies, as he opens the door to a large sitting room. "They say that this ship in unsinkable, so don't worry your pretty little self. You are entirely safe."

"But it isn't. No ship is. Actually, the *Titanic* is going to sink and thousands of the passengers are going to die. We will hit an iceberg early in the morning while everyone is sleeping." His "pretty little self" comment was condescending, and an American man in 2021 would not have said it. I felt insulted by his condescending comment.

"I have men watching for icebergs all the time, Miss Lodbrok. They do not sleep so to speak. They watch twenty-four hours a day." Then he smiles. "You American women amaze me. You are so straight forward and brash. You and Mrs. Brown make a good pair. Tell me. Did she say that you are her secretary? What exactly are your duties for Mrs. Brown?"

"Oh, the usual secretarial duties, Sir," I answer. "I must leave. I need to visit the restroom." I am ready to get out of here and back into my jeans, tee, and sweatshirt. These tight clothes and shoes are getting on my nerves. The tight waist is constricting my breathing.

"Restroom? Ah, the bath? I have one." He motions toward a doorway, and I make my way inside and lock the door. I wonder if he hears the door lock. I hope he does. The Captain's bath is large and spacious with hot and cold water, and like the rest of the ship, it is elegant. It has a Doulton lavatory basin with a marble surround. I slip the knife that I stole from the dinner table into my undergarments. I plan to keep these on no matter what the Captain's plans are.

I exit the bath and say. "The wheel room? I would like to see it."

He takes me to see the wheel room and the spectacular view of the moonlight lazily dancing on the water of the north Atlantic Ocean. The wind is very chilly and makes me shiver, and my toes hurt inside Mrs. Brown's daughter's shoes. Thinking of the sinking of the *Titanic*, makes me shiver with more chills, the kind you have when you have fever, but I know the Captain won't ever believe me, so I don't tell him. He is a poster child for arrogance. He probably thinks that I'm shivering because of him.

"Thank you. The view is wonderful, but I must retire. I think I have offended you by telling you the *Titanic* will sink, but it is the truth. It isn't a premonition. It isn't any reflection on you. Well, not really. Ah, all that wine has loosened my tongue. Actually, the *Titanic* sinks on this voyage to America."

"What are you? A fortune teller? A witch? Do not tell any other passengers on this ship your premonition, or you will cause mass hysteria." He looks angry, insulted, and is ready to be rid of me.

"Good night, Captain Smith. Until we meet again," I say and exit his cabin. I am ready to be rid of him too. I want to try out the knife on the door to the stairwell. I probably have ruined my reputation with those old money ladies by being in his cabin, but when this ship sinks, my reputation will be the last thing on their minds. They will be trying to stay afloat and to stay alive. They will be hysterical. For that matter, so will I.

"Remember, if I hear that you've been spreading gossip," he repeats, "I will have you arrested."

"You will see," I reply as I turn to leave. "Remember me, Captain Smith. Remember me."

He glares at me, and I exit. I haven't made a favorable impression on Captain Smith beyond the smell of gardenia shampoo.

Chapter 5

Without Captain Smith's help, I make my way back to the stairwell that leads below the deck. On the way, I meet one of the ladies who was at dinner. She looks away from me with a smirk on her face and otherwise doesn't acknowledge my existence by speaking. Carefully, I had hidden the lock-picking knife in my bosom. I could easily have jabbed her with it. Of course, this would get me into more trouble than I can handle right now. I think about my ancestors and wonder is violence is in my DNA. Probably, I get my temper from the Danes and the Native Americans. I retrieve the tool and looking around for others and finding no one, I unlock the door and start down the stairs. I want to return the other knife to the Irishman, so he can exit the steerage area as well when the ship begins to sink.

I meet a porter coming up the stairs. He takes note of my clothing. "Hello," he says. "Where are you going? Are you lost? Who let you inside this stairwell?"

"I need to speak to my French maid," I say. I ignore his other questions.

"Ah, I will escort you or retrieve her for you. You don't need to be down here alone. It is too dangerous with the lower class men. They are mostly drunk. What is her name?"

"There is no need. She is expecting me, and I just left the Captain, who was in distress. You should go check on him. I think it was something he ate." I say with a wink.

He looks startled at my boldness and turns to go back upstairs to check on Captain Smith.

As I reach my quarters, the French woman is waiting, but her babies are asleep. "How was your dinner? You have been gone for hours."

"Well, it tasted superb." I say. I begin taking off the clothing and shoes that Mrs. Brown has given me. I doubt that these clothes will survive the ship's sinking or a long time in the saltwater. I don't even know if the French woman and her children or I will survive either, but I will feel better if I give them to her as payment for doing my hair. I never want to owe anyone. I do know they load the lifeboats with women and children first. I remember reading that or seeing it on the movie. Of course, Captain Smith will not heed my warning. His ego is too strong. I feel somewhat better for having told him anyway. At least, I gave him something to think about. I retrieve the brown paper and twine that Mrs. Brown used and fold and wrap the clothes and shoes neatly. I use the twine to secure the package. I think again of Duct tape and wonder what year it was invented. I could have used it to secure this package instead of twine. "Here, these are for you," I say and hand her the package. I'm dressed again in my Levi jeans, tennis shoes, tee, and sweatshirt. These clothes are so comfortable. I place the lock-picking knife in my pocket again.

"Thanks for helping me do my hair. It was beautiful."

"Ah," she nods. "Thank you." She accepts the package and returns to her quarters where her children are sleeping.

I check to see that I have the Irishman's lock-picking tool securely in my pocket. I will put on the life jacket over my sweatshirt when it is time. I know that I will need to put it on in a hurry. I'm certain that this is the last time that I will see the French woman, so I say a little prayer for her and her children. I head to the General Room to return the lock-picking tool to the Irishman's pocket.

He is playing a card game with his buddies. They are laughing and having a grand time. I feel sad that he may not survive the ship's sinking, but giving him the tool back does make me feel slightly better. So I hand it to him. His buddies laugh. I kiss him on the forehead and turn to depart. "Thank you," I say. "I don't need it any more, and you may."

"What? I didn't know you had it," he says. They laugh louder.

"She is a better pick pocket than you," they jeer.

Soon, I'm back in my sleeping quarters and stretched out on my bunk. Arranging my small pillow into a more comfortable position by folding it in half and sticking it under the back of my neck, I lie down on my bunk to wait for the ship to hit the iceberg and sink. My arms are stuck under my pillow, feeling the coolness of the underside. It is a horrible feeling because I can do nothing but wait until 11:40 P.M. for the ship to hit the iceberg and all the chaos to begin. I can't remember if Captain Smith survives, but I don't think he does. I think he goes down with his ship. Well, he does in the movie. In the movie, he is holding to the wheel when he drowns. I guess my trying to tell him was like trying to change history. I think of his arrogance. I remembered being pronounced DOA at the hospital. Maybe I am a ghost. Maybe I shouldn't worry about dying whenever the ship sinks because I'm already dead. If I'm already dead, I'm really tired. I don't think dead people get tired. I look at the clock. The seconds are dragging. We begin sinking in twenty minutes. I feel helpless and frightened.

Hearing each second of the clock click by, I wait. Is this what being a ghost feels like, an eternity of waiting? I was already told that I was dead at that hospital in England. I will wait until the chaos after hitting the iceberg begins and make my way back above to the upper deck. I remember reading that some people died from jumping into the water and injuring themselves. I read about one man who broke his neck from leaping into the water. I don't intend to do that.

I make my way back into the stairwell. I unlock the door and slip outside onto the upper deck. I leave the gate open so others might exit and maybe survive. I hide in the shadows near a lifeboat. I wait. The air feels extremely cold. I am shivering again as if I have fever. Maybe I do. I feel like I'm being stuck with needles. The phantom pain in my toes hurts. Now, it has moved to my arms. I feel as if someone is trying to start an IV for drip and missing the blood vessel. My head throbs.

Suddenly, the ship hits the iceberg. There is a jerking, and the chaos begins. I know it takes a little over two hours before the *Titanic* sinks. This span of time seems to last for a week. People cry. People scream. They begin lowering the lifeboats and loading. Some leave before loaded to capacity. That is a mistake because there isn't even enough room for everyone if they were loaded to capacity.

Chapter 6

Mass hysteria and chaos happens. It is worse than it was on the movie. Loud horns sound waking people, and the ship is alive with mass confusion. I realize that we never even did a "sinking ship drill." This should be illegal. In America, disaster drills are a requirement by the government.

Although they steer away from the iceberg, the side of it pushes more holes in the hull of the *Titanic* as the ship speeds past it. Full speed ahead. Water is filling the compartments and flowing over the walls separating the watertight bulkheads. These bulkheads are the reason the ship was advertised as "unsinkable."

On the upper deck, there are only sixteen lifeboats and four collapsible boats that could accommodate only 1178 passengers. The *Titanic* has 2435 passengers, and there are 900 workers. I remember reading these statistics. People are going to die. There is no way around it. The passengers had boarded in Southhampton, England; Cherborg, France; and Queenstown, Ireland. Most of these people are high-ranking officials, wealthy industrialist, dignitaries, and celebrities. Mrs. Margaret Brown's friend John Jacob Astor, IV is also onboard. He is perhaps the wealthiest man in the world. If only arrogance could keep you alive or afloat. This may be a case of arrogance killing.

There are 700 people in third class where I had been. My ticket has only cost twenty dollars, and I am dressed like a man. I don't figure I'll get a place on a lifeboat. I am counting on Margaret Brown to help me. I must find her.

When the ship strikes the iceberg, it lurches. The warning bell rings and the engines are reversed and the ship is turned, so instead of hitting the iceberg head on, it glazes down the side with a jagged underwater spur that slashes a 300-foot gash in the hull of the ship. Within minutes, compartments fill with seawater causing the bow of the ship to be pointed downward. People slide down the shiny floors of the upper deck toward the water.

I wonder if Captain Smith has thought about my premonition now I'm certain the chaos has caused him much distress.

From what I remember, the ship has about an hour and a half before it will totally sink, so the lifeboats start being loaded. People feel death in the air. I watch the chaos as lifeboats are not loaded to full capacity. I watch Molly Brown help women and children load first. I had intended to load with her, but I can't make myself take a mother or child's place. Finally, I see Molly Brown get into one of the boats. I know that I can't change history. The chaos is rampart. People cry and wail. While loading the lifeboats women and children are separated from their husbands and fathers. It is so sad.

Finally after a couple of hours, the ship is standing on end in the ocean. I see the French woman and her toddlers clinging to each other. I take off my life jacket and hand it to her. Hurriedly, she straps it on. As I knew had to happen, I slip from the deck into the water. It is frigid. I swim away from the ship. Then the ship begins its sinking and total immersion, causing a tremendous whirlpool. I along with all the others near the ship, am sucked under the water in a swirl around the ship. How can I drown? I'm already dead. I feel my lungs fill with water. The smell and taste is fishy, and it feels like ice water. I grab onto a wooden headboard nearby and hang on. It should float back to the surface. Maybe soon, someone will rescue me. All of us. I wonder if I'm really already dead or if I'm going to drown now. I don't understand the pain I feel in my airways. I don't understand the pressure I feel in my head. I don't understand how I can think, taste, and smell, but not breathe.

The wooden headboard allows me to rise to the surface after the ship sinks deeper into the freezing water. The headboard floats, and I float on it in the frigid water. My fingers lose all their circulation. I wait. I hear rescue boats picking up the survivors in the lifeboats. I see dead bodies floating in the water. Using my hood laces, I tie myself to the wooden headboard. Slowly in the cold water, soon I am semi-conscious. I know that I was already dead, but still I wait to be rescued. I think of my DNA results. I suppose this trip on the *Titanic* is the 15% English part of my DNA results. What a way to experience it.

I float on the freezing water tied to the headboard. I wait. Everyone else disappears. The current is taking me away from the others. I wait to see where I will land next, or if I will die or am already really dead. I hope the French woman that I gave the life jacket and her toddlers are rescued and didn't stay in the freezing water too long. Actually, I hope she got into one of the lifeboats I'm certain that I no longer smell of gardenias nor want to. I know from reading history that Margaret Brown survives. I know that I can't change history.

Finally, I wake from my semi-conscious state, or do I. I feel like I did after the car accident in England when I was pronounced DOA. I feel like I'm watching the events of my life as a movie. I feel like I'm floating above myself, but I'm actually floating in the fishy smelling water. The water becomes slightly warmer, but not much. I am still freezing. I'm shivering like someone with fever. I try to make myself quit shivering, but I can't. I hear a strange noise. Ice crystals have formed on my hair. It makes a crunching sound when I move my head, like I'm wearing beads in it. I look up into the sunshine, but it isn't warm enough to melt the ice crystals. Inhaling hurts. My head aches. I hadn't expected to ever see the sunshine again. I look around. No one else is floating near me. The sound I hear is from oars being dipped into the water. A ship with a large carved dragon and a tall sail is headed toward me. I try to call out, but my voice is hoarse and mostly gone. It comes out as a tiny squeak like an insect. The sound of the oars lapping the water stops, and the carved dragon ship floats near me. They are beside me. Arms reach out. My laces that tie me to the wooden headboard are cut. I am drawn onboard. Once again, I'm rescued. I am not dead. Or am I?

"Well, lookie here," I hear. "It is a girl. I have found me a slave girl," a smallish man with black eye make-up and dragon tatoos on his arms says. The tatoos make me think of America, but this boat definitely does not. Although I know what he says, he isn't speaking English. I don't know how I understand him.

Through half-closed lids I peer at my rescuer. I am so tired and cold. He doesn't look to be English or American. He reminds me of a character I saw on television in the television show The Vikings. He has sparse, gray hair on the top of his head, the dark tatoos of lightening bolts and arrows cover all of his face, and he has dripping black eye make-up that may be a tatoo too. I must be dreaming. Those lightening bolts become popular again in 2022. But I don't think these people are from 2022. I hear someone address him as Floke. The man on The Vikings television show was named Floke too. He wraps me in a warm, dry woolen blanket that smells musty and like the fishy water, and lays me on the deck of the ship. My hair has begun to thaw. I am lulled to sleep by the sound of the oars dipping into the water. I am exhausted and still shiver with cold, but drift back into a sleepy, exhausted state after finally getting warmer from the fishy smelling blanket. I have been rescued. I wonder if I'm dead. I may be, but I don't think I am. Although I want to go to Heaven, I hope this isn't Heaven. I don't really think that I'm dead yet. I think I too survived the *Titanic*.

When I awake, we have reached land. I'm bound tightly with leather cords and escorted to what I think is Floke's camp that consists of houses with covered-roofs and dirt and dried vegetation like hay. Some have green vegetation growing on their roofs. The air here smells like that musty blanket that I had on his ship. There are several out-buildings made of the same materials with the same roofs. It is a primitive village and much more primitive that anything I've seen before even at Native American museums. I had seen pictures of the Vikings on television, in books, and online. There is a woman and a small child at his camp, and apparently Floke has other slaves besides me. I see some older men and women and some young girls. I don't see many young men. His camp is near a larger camp of people that I assume are Danish too. I suppose this is the main village. So I really don't know for sure that these other people are his slaves.

I think I'm now the slave of a Viking man and his wife. He seems amused by me, but his wife seems to hate me. Anyway, she is definitely not amused. So, I am not really dead or am I. I am directed to a large, wooden tub of water and an oily, soapy product to wash. I must stink like the ocean water. The smell of the soap is definitely not gardenias, but I'm glad to get to bathe. The slats of the tub are held together by iron bands. The iron bands feel cold to my toes and back. The water hasn't been heated much, but it is a little above room temperature. It is warmer than the ocean water was. Although I'd been floating in the ocean for a while, maybe hours or days. I'm not certain, I know a bath will make me feel better, but I don't think I will ever enjoy swimming again. The clothes I'm given to wear must have belonged to Floke's wife. She is about my size. The undergarments are made of linen. Here I go again putting on someone else's underwear and clothes. The linen fabric feels soft. They look hand sewn.

The outer clothes- a tunic and a skirt -are made of wool. It feels itchy. I have never liked wearing woolen clothing, but here I will take whatever is offered. Perhaps the linen undergarments will help keep the wool away from my skin and prevent chafing.

Although I'm exhausted, I wash and clean myself. Feeling as if someone is watching me the entire time, I dress quickly in Floke's wife's clothes. I have a long dress with long sleeves and an apron made of wool which is appropriate for this cold temperature. The linen keeps the wool away from my bare skin. I overhear an intense conversation between Floke and his wife while I comb out the tangles in my hair, but I don't understand what they are saying. I don't exactly understand their language. My hair is matted and tangled. It hasn't been combed since the French woman fixed it for me whenever I was invited to eat with Captain Smith. I think that was only yesterday, but it feels like it was a month ago. I listen to these people's conversation. I think their language is Danish. I think of my DNA results that I'm 25 % Danish. I wonder what Audrey would have to say about this adventure. I wonder if she is out of college and already married. I don't think this is 2022 or 1912. I wonder what year this is. I wonder if I'm alive or dead. I think I'm alive, but I also think I'm in trouble.

Once I'm dressed in Floke's wife's clothes, I walk to where he and his wife are. "My name is Heidi Lodbrok," I say patting myself to indicate that I am Heidi. I pronounce my name *HiDee LoadBrok*. She gives me a disbelieving look. She wears a woolen tunic with a linen tunic under it similar to what I'm wearing. It that falls to her mid thigh. Her legs are shapely from hard work. The one I am wearing covers more skin. Long leggings are worn with the tunic because it is cold here. What I'm wearing is hand made too. Floke calls her Geishala.

Floke and Geishala look at each other in a strange way. There eyes communicate something, but I don't understand what. It must be something that I said.

"Lodbrok?" Floke asks. He has an astonished look on his face. "You know Ragnar Lodbrok?"

"No," I shake my head. "I'm from America."

"Amer, America? I'm going into the village to get Ragnar."

"No," his wife says. "Heidi is our slave. Ragnar will take her away from us."

"She belongs to us. He will have to pay us if he takes her," Floke says. "I rescued her. She is mine."

"Ours. She will take care of the baby Aud and help me spin wool and cook and clean."

It sounded as if I truly was destined to be a working slave no matter where I was. "My daughter's name is Audrey. We often call her Aud." I say, but they don't understand anything but the word Aud and perhaps Audrey.

Floke and Geishala look at each other again. "You will be our governess." He rocks his arms like rocking a baby and points to her. Geishala picks up my long, blond wet hair that I've combed to remove the tangles and let dry.

"This hair will have to go," Geishala says. "Slaves can't have long hair. It is too much trouble. I will cut it."

"Her hair will stay. I like it," Floke says and giggles. "I'm her master. She's my slave girl. She must do as I say, and so must you." He giggles again. "You are my wife."

"Our slave," Geishala says. "She is our slave, not just yours, and when do I do what you say?"

"I think that she needs to be taught to be a shield maiden to go raiding with us. We are going to raid Mercia (England) next. Rollo says. Then we may go with Leif Erickson on a trip west, perhaps even to America. Ragnar wants to go to the Mediterranean, too. We need all the warriors that we can get. So far, we have a few hundred men and women. They live in the village. I have begun to build ships for the raiding for Rollo, Ragnar, and Leif. We were testing one when we found Heidi the slave girl." He pronounces my name *HiDee*.

"What will you do if Ragnar claims her after she has been trained to be a shield maiden? He needs warriors too. Maybe he doesn't need to know that her name is Lodbrok. She can't speak our language yet. She can't tell."

"I'm more worried about Rollo. He isn't married like Ragnar. And he likes slave women. He likes them too much. He can't understand her language, but he will know if she says Lodbrok."

I look around the room. The underside of a straw roof is visible from the underside and the roof supports are visible. It is primitive. There is a smoky smell from the center fire. I look for an opening for the smoke to escape. I don't see one. This is the long house, and there is an open hearth in the middle of the floor. I remember from watching The Vikings on television. Actually, I watched all six seasons of The Vikings on Sunday nights on The History Channel. It was one of my favorite television programs. Well-worn benches are set up surrounding the hearth. They are smooth to the touch. It looks as if they serve as seats or couches. The hearth contains glowing hot coals. Long, low tables sit over to the side near primitive tools that appear to be for spinning, weaving, and use on wool. Large bone combs are stuck in the wool. It looks like they are used to comb the wool straight before spinning it into yarn. It is toasty warm in here, but I am still chilled from floating in the sea for so long. I move closer to the fire. I really thought I was going to drown in that cold water or die from the cold, frigid temperature of the water, but I didn't. I don't think that I will ever be warm again.

Then I notice the kitchen. Of course, there is no electricity here. I see large wooden troughs, pails, and even vats that are reinforced with iron hoops. They are hanging on racks and stacked on low tables. Nearby are spoons and ladles. I see meat cleavers, axes, handmade knives and grilling forks. These are meat-eating people. These have been stuck in some pails. I see roasting pits and kettles. I see other pans made of soapstone. Over to one side is an iron kettle hanging on an iron tripod. I see a large millstone. This kitchen is well-stocked, but all this looks primitive to me but I don't care. To me, all cooking is work. Using primitive utensils will make it harder to do. I actually am used to eating fast food at home. I smell food. It is a meaty stew. I am famished. I haven't eaten since last night when we dined with Captain Smith on the *Titanic*, and I was too nervous to eat much. I remember his arrogance. I hate arrogance. I told him the ship was going to sink. Of course, he didn't believe me. I wiggle my toes. They still feel strange. Since my car wreck in England, my toes have tingled.

"It is time to eat," Geishala says. Her tone of voice isn't inviting. "I will teach our slave to clean up after dinner. Floke, will you go get the pot of stew and set it on the long table? It is heavy. Our slave is still weak."

There is a knock on the door and a tall, muscular man walks inside. He is gorgeous. He has not waited for an invitation to enter. He must have smelled the food too. It could be like a dinner bell because it really smells wonderful.

"I heard about the new slave. A woman?" a man says.

He looks directly into my eyes with eyes as deep as the ocean where I had floated into the Viking world. "I'm Rollo. Who are you?" Rollo asks. Since my husband was named Lodbrok, his friends had called him Rollo after The Vikings' television show as a nickname. It had been a joke, but he didn't look anything like Rollo.

I admire his red hair, but say nothing. I nod and smile. The way he is looking at me, I think I will suffocate. I can't catch my breath. I haven't ever felt this way before. I feel as if someone needs to put something like oxygen over my mouth and nose to help me breathe. His stares are worse than being underwater for too long, or maybe they are better. I can feel that he thinks I'm attractive, too.

"This is my new slave, Heidi," Floke says. He pronounces my name HiDee again. He doesn't say Lodbrok. I gather Lodbrok is a secret since he doesn't want Ragnar Lodbrok to take me away from him.

"Our slave," Geishala adds. She glares at me, daring me to open my mouth, so I don't because she controls me now as does her husband, Floke. They are my food, clothing, and shelter.

"She can't speak for herself," Rollo asks, giving me an approving once-over look. "I'd like to get to know her a lot better if you know what I mean. Hello, my name is Rollo."

"If she is female, you are the same way with each of them. Tonight, I'm teaching her to do kitchen work and to take care of our changeling baby, Aud."

I look up at the mention of the baby's name. I don't know exactly what a changeling baby is. I have read about changelings. But, I don't think it is good. Rollo seems to cringe at the word changeling.

I look at Geishala and smile. I fold my arms into a rocking the baby gesture and raise my eyebrows. She nods and then I follow Geishala. We leave the room to get the baby that Geishala has called a changeling.

Baby Aud is sleeping when we enter her room, but when Geishala lifts her from her cradle and hands her to me, I feel fever burning the child's skin, and her nose is stuffy, and she is pink around her eyes like she has a cold.

"She is sick," I say. "She has fever. We need to get her fever down. Do you have any medicine for fever? And she's congested. She needs to inhale some steam." I indicate the congestion with my hands near my nose, and I know that there is no aspirin, Tylenol, or pharmacy here.

"Cornflower tea is for fever?" Gieshala says.

"I don't know about cornflower tea, but we need to bathe her in cold water and perhaps alcohol to bring her fever down quickly," I say. I am wishing for some liquid Tylenol. I bundle Aud in some of her bed clothes and follow Geishala back into the other main building with her.

When we reenter, another man is sitting with Floke and Rollo.

"This is Heidi, my slave. I picked her up in the sea water whenever I was trying out one of my new ships. She doesn't speak our language."

Rollo and Ragnar, Floke indicates toward me. "Ragnar," I acknowledge.

"She seems to understand more that you realize," Ragnar says. "Perhaps we can make a shield maiden of her. She looks somewhat fit and intelligent. She doesn't seem frightened of us. You say you found her floating in the sea. We need many more shield maidens when we go raiding. We have many plans for raiding in the spring. Geishala, what do you say to that?"

"I need a baby nurse," Geishala replies, "and a kitchen slave."

"We will see. When you have taught her to cook, spin, and tend babies, what will you do with your time? You do not wish to be a shield maiden yourself. Do you? You have said as much. We definitely need more shield maidens and warriors. I repeat, whenever we raid Mercia, we will need more warriors. She looks strong enough to be a raider and a warrior."

"She probably can do both," Floke says. "She can work in the kitchen, tend to Aud, and learn to be a shield maiden too."

"Now, we are tending to our sick baby Aud. Heidi says that Aud has a high fever. She is preparing a treatment. We are giving her cornflower tea and cold compresses for the fever."

They looked toward the kitchen to see me steeping cornflower tea and searching for a bottle of alcohol and some honey.

Audrey

"When will my mother wake up?" Audrey asks the English doctor. "When can I take her back to America to a hospital in Memphis?"

"I would prefer that she be conscious before she is flown to America, but I do not know when that will be. No one can have any way of knowing."

"Can I take her while she is unconscious?"

"Yes, but a qualified nurse will have to accompany her. Can you afford that? It will be very expensive."

"Can I have my own nurse from America fly with us?"

The doctor looks at me as if he doesn't know what to do with me as if I'm a headstrong American which I am. Then he simply says, "Yes."

Chapter 7

"Drink your mead, Ragnar. She isn't going anywhere. She was floating in the sea. She was semi-conscious. She isn't leaving because she has nowhere to go." He looks directly at Rollo. "She is our slave."

"I noticed that she isn't tied up," Rollo answers.

His eyes caress me again. I notice that he is wearing a linen tunic with woolen leggings underneath. I notice his muscular legs. I notice that his body is muscular and strong. Ragnar is the same, but his hair is blond like mine, and he wears it braided tightly to his scalp. Compared to Floke, Ragnar and Rollo are muscle men on steroids.

I bathe Aud in wine and cool water with a cloth. I give her three spoons of cornflower tea made from cornflower leaves steeped in water. I hope that isn't too much. I've never heard of cornflower tea as a fever reducer, but I know aspirin is made from bark of a tree. After about thirty minutes, the fever lessens and Aud sits up and gazes around the room. There is no clock here to know exactly what time it is. Aud coos and giggles baby talk at us. It is clear that she feels better, but her eyes are still glassy from the sickness.

Geishala says, "Ragnar and Rollo, sup with us. We have dried fish, stew, and apples cooked in honey." She sets a flask of mead and horns on the table. This sounds like organic food or Weight Watchers to me. It sounds delicious, and I am starving. It is definitely not fast food or processed. Organic food is not usually my first choice.

"Awe, my favorite," Ragnar replies, studying me much in the same way that Rollo had, making me feel self-conscious. American men aren't as obvious with their looking at women. These two would be terrible poker players because their faces give their thoughts and intentions away. They definitely don't have poker faces.

I help Geishala warm the evening meal over the fire and set it of the long wooden table. Finally, I am getting a little warmer. I know a full stomach of warm food will warm me more. I wonder if the stew is fresh. It smells great. There is no refrigerator, but I think it is kept warm for days to keep it from spoiling, making the flavors melt together. More is added to it each day. I'm so hungry that I plan to eat it with them. Not having a refrigerator hasn't killed them yet. After all there aren't any fast food restaurants here, and I have no money. Anyway, they are still alive and not sick. Large kegs of honey mead are set within easy reach of the guests at the table. Everyone begins eating at once except me. I wait for a prayer or something as I do at home. There is none. These people are not Christian. If they raid Mercia (England,) they will find Protestants or Catholics. They aren't either. They are Danish pagans. I remember from The Vikings shows on television.

Rollo pours me a large horn full of honey mead and motions for me to drink. I take a sip and find the taste sweet and inviting, so I drink the entire horn quickly. As soon as that one is drunk, Rollo pours me another one. Before the honey mead has run out,

I have drunk as many horns as Rollo, matching him horn for horn. Yet, I don't feel inebriated. Ordinarily, I am not much of a drinker, but I love this drink. I feel like I have been drinking it all my life.

Geishala seems jealous of my ability to drink and of how the men are fascinated with me. "Can I stay overnight?" Rollo asks me. "And share your bed?"

Watching his eyes, I understand the jest of his question, but refuse his offer. "I don't understand your customs," I say, "but where I come from, we don't sleep over." I knew I was lying because America's morals in 2022 weren't prudish at all, "I don't know you that well." I say and laugh aloud. Then I remember Captain Smith from the *Titanic*. At least Rollo isn't totally arrogant like Captain Smith, but he seems a little arrogant and confident.

As if that was exactly what Geishala wanted to hear, she smiles. "She is our slave, Rollo. She does what we say, and she is not for sale."

"We share," Ragnar says, moving his arm in a motion to include everyone and indicating polygamy. I notice that Floke is happy that I turned Rollo's invitation down too, and Geishala was not going to change her mind.

I help Geishala clear the table of uneaten food and fish bones, but the men never stop drinking honey mead and don't seem to get drunk. I also noticed that their table manners lack a lot of training. For instance, belching loudly. Finally, a few minutes before midnight Ragnar leaves, but Rollo stays. I wonder where he will sleep. Perhaps on one of the long benches at the table. I don't intend for him to sleep in my bed.

Even after he had said that he wouldn't tell him, Floke explains to Rollo that Lodbrok is my last name.

"I don't believe you," Rollo says. "Where is she from? I thought you said America. Where is America? In the west? How can she be a Lodbrok?"

"Far across the ocean," I reply. "In a different time and place."

"Don't tell Ragnar that her last name is Lodbrok," Floke asks of Rollo. "I found her floating in the sea clinging to a large piece of wooden furniture that I didn't recognize. It was ornate. I don't think that she floated all the way from America. Leif Erickson says that is a very long trip. He says it takes days to get there. She probably was in the water for hours not days. She is my slave girl," Floke insists and giggles in his nervous characteristic way. It is the same way the character Floke on The Vikings on television giggled.

"Let's teach her to be a shield maiden," Rollo says in a serious tone.

Floke nods to Rollo and taking the shield from the wall where it hangs shows me one of his shields. It is round, wooden, and has a wooden-shaped X painted across it. It is very heavy. "I will make her a shield," Floke says. "She can train and also help me build my ships. That will help her get stronger to be a shield maiden."

"I want you to build me a fleet of ships," Rollo says. "For me only. Not for Ragnar. Ragnar is the lord of this land, but I want to go raiding the Anglo Saxton countries of Mercia, Northumbria, and France and conquer another land for myself to be lord of it by myself not with him. That is my wish. My dream. I will buy her a sword and train her myself."

"That's a long time in the future. A fleet of ships takes some time to build, so in the meantime, she can train, work on the ships, and help Geishala. All that work will make her strong."

Suddenly Geishala bursts into the room. "Aud's fever is raging again. She is a changeling. I just know it. We must give her back to the fairies tonight. We need them to bring our healthy child back and take this sickly fairy child."

"It is the gods who want Aud. If she isn't better tomorrow night, we will place her outside as a changeling. We don't want to anger the gods." Floke sounds adamant. His tone of voice says not to argue. So no one does.

Rollo and Floke head to the sleeping quarters of the long house, and I begin trying to lower Aud's fever again with another bath of cool water, more cornflower tea, and three spoons of honey. Finally, Aud's fever is lowered. I wish for a thermometer to know exactly how high her fever gets, but of course, there is no emergency room here to carry her to. I place Aud in her bed, and the sweet baby goes back to sleep. I am so tired from floating in the sea after the *Titanic* sunk and being found by these Danish people that I want to crawl into bed with the baby and sleep for a week.

Geishala shows me where I will sleep, but as I get undressed, Geishala invites me into the bed with her and Floke.

"No," I answer, shaking my head. I don't understand these Danish customs of polygamy. "I will stay in here near Aud and sleep." I don't understand Geishala's invitation because clearly she is jealous and vengeful. She seems more jealous of Rollo and me than of Floke and me. I remember Ragnar's statement about sharing, but it is not my custom.

I get into bed alone and pull the animal hides up around my chin. There is still a faint animal smell to them, but they feel soft and warm. I'm so tired. I am homesick for my on daughter Audrey and wonder if she is married yet. I think about the sinking of the *Titanic*. I think about my car accident, hitting my head, and my tingling toes. I wonder how many people survived on the *Titanic*. I forgot how many the newspapers reported. I wonder if the French woman who fixed my hair for my dinner with Margaret Brown and the Captain was a survivor. I wonder if her two toddlers survived. I wonder if I will ever know. I wonder if they got into a life boat as women and children were loaded first, but probably not those considered the lower class women and children. I wonder about Margaret Brown. From reading history and newspaper accounts, I already know that Molly Brown survives. Knowing things that are going to happen is a strange feeling. I think about being rescued by Floke, and the difference in time. The *Titanic* sank in 1912. This is 994. I think about my own daughter Audrey getting married in 2021 or 2022 and about her grieving, thinking her mother is dead. I try to wriggle my toes. They are still very cold. I can't wait to crawl into my bed and sleep.

Then I think about becoming a shield maiden. The thought excites me. Previously in America, I wore my hair in a shield maiden style after I watched The Vikings, now I have the opportunity to be an actual shield maiden in an actual Danish fight. I really don't know how to get back to America from here. I especially don't know how to get back to 2022 from 994.

Finally, I get cozy and warm and drop off to sleep. It is as if my mind is in a fog. I am awakened by the ailing baby, Aud, who is crying. I am certain that she feels bad. Fever has a way of making you feel really bad. I get up and pick Aud up out of her bed, taking her into the kitchen closer to the fire. I give her more cornflower tea and honey. Apparently, the cornflower tea only lowers fever for a few hours. Perhaps the antibiotic property of the honey will get rid of the infection causing her fever, and if she has a virus, I don't think the honey will hurt her. When I return to my bed, Rollo is in it, but he is sound asleep and snoring loudly. I'm not sure where he was sleeping before. I place Aud in the bed next to him. The baby snuggles in next to him, and I get in next to her on the other side. He has warmed the entire bed making it very comfortable, but his snoring doesn't make sleeping easy for me. I remember that Audrey's father John used to snore and that in America after he left, I often felt lonely. I feel lonely now.

In the early morning, I wake to Rollo leaning on one elbow and staring at me.

"If Floke puts her out as a changeling, she will die," Rollo says, motioning toward Aud. "I will get different baby clothes, and he moves with his hands to indicate what he is saying. We will go get her and change her into a different gown. They will not know she is the same baby. You must help me," Rollo says.

"I will," I reply, liking Rollo more than ever because of his tender heart toward Aud, and for only sleeping in my bed and keeping us warm. I even forgive his snoring.

We all three fall asleep again, but Geishala wakes us later in the morning. She is displeased that the baby is asleep in our bed. Or she is displeased about something. I can't be certain what. Nothing I have done so far has made her like me. I don't think she ever will.

"Odin and Thor will be angry," Geishala says to Rollo. "You must go." She doesn't seem as concerned for Aud as I think she should be. She baffles me. She quickly leaves the room.

Rollo rises and stumbles around finding his woolen leggings and dressing. Then he winks at me and leaves. "I will be back tonight," he says. "We will begin training you tomorrow to be a shield maiden. I will bring you a sword." I don't understand his staying here uninvited.

I smile at him. I have begun to understand some of what he says. "Aud seems better this morning," I say. "I would have snuggled with my own sick child."

"Changeling," Geishala replies, taking the baby to the other room while I dress. "Hurry up, we must spin lots of wool into yarn today."

Chapter 8

"I will be right there," I say. I quickly dress in the same clothes I wore yesterday. I'm certain that they smell and there is no deodorant here. Geishala is wearing the same dress with a woolen apron over it. I wonder how long a Danish person here wears the same clothing. As in how many days. I wonder how they launder or clean the wool clothes, or if they do. There is no Febreeze here, and no place to purchase it or anything like it, but I think that they do have a market in the town. I bet they only launder their linen undergarments and wear the wool ones for a few days before they air them. I think about all the smoke. The clothing should have a smoky smell. I know that some people in the village are merchants, some peasants, some explorers and sea farers, some pirates or traders, some craftsmen, some killers, and some artists. And then there is Floke who builds ships. He seems to be one-of-a-kind here or the only ship builder.

They eat a spicy grain mush for breakfast prepared by someone that I haven't seen before, and after breakfast we begin at once to spin the wool into yarn while that other woman who made the mush cleans. I wonder where she was last night.

That woman is very old. I think, but I am not certain. She doesn't seem as well-cared for as Geishala does. If I stay here as a slave, I may look like her too after a few years. My daddy would have called it "rode hard and put up wet" look. It wasn't a compliment.

I catch on quickly to spinning wool as if it is something I had done many times. I remember the ancestry test and the results saying I was of Danish decent. Geishala shows me a finished sweater and short skirt. I'm not sure about knitting yet. "This is for a special occasion," Geishala says, holding it up to her body. She adds a necklace with a box hanging on it that rests on her breasts. I have a vague feeling of having seen it in a picture before. Maybe I saw it online. I remember the way the women on the *Titanic* dressed. This is so very different. I actually like this better. They aren't as snobbish, and the clothes look more comfortable.

I remember that Geishala truly thinks baby Aud is a changeling. I do not understand, but I have read about changelings, but I don't believe in them. I hope Rollo can help. I'm not certain that I can leave that baby outside in the cold temperature at night. To me that is child abuse or just psychotic to leave her out with all the wild animals.

All day long, I feel like Geishala shuns Aud. She doesn't pick her up, give her cornflower tea, or feed her, but when Geishala isn't looking or is outside, I do. I can't help myself. I feel so sorry for Aud. She is a beautiful little girl who has a cold or an ear infection as most children do at that age.

Rollo returns later in the middle of the day with a sword and shield for me. We move outdoors. He gives me the first instructions and begins my shield maiden training. "Hold it by the handle and learn the feel of its weight," he instructs. "Swing it over your head until you get used to the weight of it and build your strength. Make it become an extension of your arm." He swings it over his own head to show me what he means.

I follow his instructions over and over again until the sword feels more natural in my hands. I wonder if when the time comes to fight, I can really do it. I'm certain fighting is an adrenaline rush, but I don't think I could kill anyone.

"I don't care if you teach her to be a shield maiden," Geishala says, "but I am going to want her to help me with chores here like spinning, cooking, taking care of the baby, tending fires, and cleaning." I cringe at Geishala's words. She seems to really hate me, and I don't know why. It can't be because I'm weak as that is the reason she doesn't seem to love Aud. I am very strong, even stronger than she is. I am a survivor. I doubt she would have survived the sinking of the *Titanic*. Again, I wonder is the French woman with the two toddlers survived. I pray they did. I hope they got into a lifeboat and were rescued.

"When Floke finishes our fleet of boats, we are going raiding in Mercia or France. Probably we will go next spring after the ice and snow thaws. You can come too, Geishala, if you want to," Rollo says. His flaming red hair touches his shoulders, and he looks very charming. I notice that his hair is freshly shampooed, but it doesn't smell of perfume. I would like to know what he used to shampoo it because it shines like a new penny.

Geishala doesn't agree to going raiding, but I am excited for the adventure. In a way, I'm glad that she doesn't want to go. My only problem is leaving Aud, or more specifically, leaving Aud with her.

"Heidi must help with building of the fleet too. She can peel the bark off the logs," Floke says. "She can use the bark spud. It will strengthen her muscles for holding the shield and swinging the sword. Most of my other slaves are too old and weak to help. She is the youngest and strongest slave that I have."

Geishala grunts as if I disgust her.

I notice the jealousy, close to hatred, that Geishala has toward me, but I don't know what to do to stop it because I don't know what I did to cause it. Finally, I determine that I didn't do anything. As soon as Geishala and Floke leave the room, I whisper with hand motions and ask Rollo if he is helping me tonight to rescue Aud.

"Yes," he nods.

So as usual the baby's fever spikes at bed time, so I slip Aud some cornflower tea with lots of honey and bathe her head with cold compresses, and I dress her warmly because I don't know what time they plan to take her outside into the cold to exchange her for their baby that they think fairies took. She is tucked into her crib for the night. Instead of leaving her in her crib to sleep, Floke scoops her up and takes her out to the two, hollow, forked trees. Rollo and I follow, but Geishala remains in the long house. Her unconcern about the baby bothers me tremendously. It is child neglect. Floke wraps Aud in a blanket and leaves her as a changeling for the fairies to exchange for Floke and Geishala's healthy baby. They go back to the house and wait for an exchange. Rollo and I follow Floke. I memorize the way to the two, hollow, forked trees, so that I can return.

Thank goodness he has placed her up high enough to be somewhat safe. Well, safer than she would be on the ground.

"The god's will rescue her after the fairies bring her back," Floke says. "It is their way. I spoke with Odin and he told me so. He says that two wolves are in my future not two ravens. If the fairies don't bring our baby back and this baby dies, our baby will have gone to Valhalla. Odin says we are not to have a wake or a feast if the changeling dies." I cringe at what he says. The unconcern for this child really bothers me.

I think of St. Jude, the children's hospital in Memphis. I wonder what they would think of the Danish way of leaving a sick child out in the cold for the fairies. I wonder how many weak and sick children survive this ordeal. Then I think about the television show The Vikings and how the infant Ivar was crippled and left out to die, but was rescued.

After we reach the long house, Geishala seems more and more unconcerned to me. She doesn't even ask about the location of where Floke left Aud. She almost seems glad to be rid of Aud. It really bothers me. Floke tells her that he has followed Odin's directions about the changeling. I feel Rollo stiffen next to me, but he doesn't say anything. Neither do I. We just wait.

We have left baby Aud in the hollow of the two trees grown into one and walked back to the village. I am so concerned for Aud being out in the woods alone that I can't eat any of my food. I must help Geishala clean and put away the food, but I can't think of anything to talk to her about. I keep my mouth shut. Slaves aren't required to talk. Soon, I go to my sleeping area and retire for the night. I can't sleep, but hear the noises and conversation from the other room. I listen for cries from Aud, but I don't hear any. I wonder if she if too far away or if she is sleeping. I rise and place a large stone near the fire to warm. This is how my grandmother warmed her bed by warming a brick and wrapping it in a towel. Then she placed it in her bed near her feet. I used an electric blanket or an electric heating pad on the cold nights or whenever I had aches and pains.

Rollo keeps pouring honey mead for Floke and Geishala. Finally, after numerous horns, Floke and Geishala go to their bed area. Rollo slips into the bedroom with me. "When they are asleep, we will slip outside to where Aud is in those forked trees," he whispers and motions with his hands. "The excess mead should help them sleep soundly." Then he reaches under my bed and takes out the package of alternate baby clothes to put on Aud. He opens the package and shows me the clothing. It is a woolen baby dress. "If they find her in different clothing, they will think she is a different child and that the fairies took Aud."

I just hope she is still alive and not sicker when we go to change her clothing. I plan to go as soon as possible. I hope Floke didn't mark Aud in some way. Geishala seemed so unconcerned I know she didn't. He needs to believe that this is a different baby too. If she isn't sick, I don't think Geishala will care. I wonder if Geishala had another baby before that they thought was a changeling. Or perhaps one of her siblings was thought to be a changeling.

After the house is quiet, Rollo sneaks to Floke and Geishala's bedding area and determines them to be sound asleep. The excess honey mead has done its job. Actually, it makes you sleepy instead of inebriated. To me, that is about the same.

"Let's go," he motions to me. We take the different baby clothing that Rollo brought. He has brought a linen dress and a woolen jacket and woolen leggings. We sneak outside to the forked tree where Aud is. Rollo takes her down, and I change Aud's clothing and stuff the clothes she was wearing inside my shirt. Luckily, the weather wasn't as cold as it had been on previous nights, but I slip the warmed stone wrapped in cloth in with Aud inside the hollow tree to help keep her warm until tomorrow. I give her more cornflower tea and honey. As much as I don't like it, we leave Aud in the opening of the hollow trees. She has to be there when Floke comes to get her as the changeling. I make certain to put her up high enough for most wild dogs not to be able to reach her, but I know that there are other wild animals that can climb trees in the forest. There could be bobcats, panthers, opossums, raccoons, in addition to the wild dogs. I don't care what Floke thinks about the higher position in the trees. Aud's safety comes first. Floke will know that she couldn't have gotten higher in the tree by herself, but the fairies could have moved her.

As we make our way down the snow-covered path back to the sleeping house, Rollo tells me that a changeling grows uglier in appearance and behavior as it matures which isn't the case with Aud. Rollo says that the changelings are sickly, ill-featured, malformed and ill-tempered. I think about the commercials on television of children with cleft pallets. Rollo says that it screams and bites and scratches. He shows me a scar on the top of his hand where he was scratched. The changeling is supposed to be very cunning.

I wonder if he truly believes in the fairies and changelings or not. It really seems that he does. At least he is helping save baby Aud. Finally, I decide that for some reason, Rollo doesn't trust what Odin, one of their gods, says. I know that I don't.

As the night goes on, I can't sleep for worrying about Aud. I slip out of the house to check on the baby, but find her sound asleep in the hollow, forked trees. I touch the warming stone. It is still warm. So I sneak back into the sleeping room and into the bed beside Rollo, who is already snoring loudly. I am relieved that he is snoring.

I am beginning to like Rollo more and more. He has a kind soul with a tender heart, and he is very good-looking in a rugged kind of way. I fall into a light sleep, but I dream of being in a hospital in America. I dream that my breathing is restricted, and I can't feel my toes. I dream that Audrey and her boyfriend are standing over my bed. Audrey is trying to get me to wake up from a long sleep of unconsciousness after an accident. In my dream, I don't actually know what kind of accident, but she sings a lullaby to me, one that I used to sing to her when she was a baby.

Early the next morning, Floke goes back to the hollow trees and finds a happy, cheerful baby. Geishala says, "The fairies brought my baby back. This is really Aud. It is not the sickly changeling. Look how they dressed her."

Rollo and I look at each other. We are relieved, especially me. It is hard not to jump for joy. So this baby had been replaced according to Geishala. Only Rollo and I know that it is actually the same child in different clothing. Floke hasn't mentioned the warming stone. I think he knows, but I hope he doesn't ever mention the warming stone to Geishala. He didn't return it when he picked up Aud. Anyway, the fairies could have placed it there. Fairies are like that.

Once we are back at the house with Aud, Geishala asks to place the child in a hot oven as a further test of whether it is Floke and her baby or not, but Rollo convinces her that if it had not been her child back from the fairies, it would not have been dressed differently. She agrees, but says, "Both the changeling baby and our baby Aud have a birthmark on its back in the same location. How unusual is that? She takes the baby and tucks it into its own crib instead of placing it in the oven.

I sigh a sigh of relief, but cringe at the beliefs Geishala has about babies and hope that this nightmare of Aud being a changeling is over. I am surprised that any Danish children ever survive. I look at Rollo with love for helping me save Aud. Although he looks bold and brash with his fiery-colored, curly locks, and scraggily beard, his heart is tender for children, especially babies. I want to tell him *thank you for saving Aud*, but the language barrier stops me. "Teach me to speak your language," I ask and motion with my hands.

"I will," Rollo nods and turns his group of bracelets around and around on his upper arm. I reach up under his chin and loosen the fasteners that hold his cloak. Then I hug him to me. Suddenly Floke and Geishala enter the room. I hang Rollo's cloak on an iron hook near the door, but Floke is dressed to go out into the cold. "Heidi can help us begin working on the ships today. She can peel the bark off the logs. Her arms will get stronger quickly if she peels bark and stacks logs. Then she will be better at spinning." He gives his characteristic giggle.

"I need her here this morning to help with the baby and to help spin wool," Geishala says, decisively. "She can't help you today."

I look at Rollo, who grabs his cloak and follows Floke toward the door. He doesn't argue with her. Somehow, I feel that Floke knows the changeling or Aud is the same baby, but as long as Geishala is satisfied, he says nothing. He especially doesn't mention Odin or Thor again, and Gieshala really never has. I wonder about his belief in Odin and Thor, but don't dare ask him. I can't imagine having gods who are real people that you can go up on a mountain to a temple and talk to. They wouldn't survive in America. Their gods don't live in heaven or their Valhalla.

"We will cut the trees and pile them for you to peel," he says to me. "Rollo will show you what to do and how to use the bark spud. This morning you help Geishala." I didn't know whether I had rather help Geishala spin wool or go out into the cold to peel bark off logs, but I was glad to stay inside where it was warm with Aud who seemed to be over her sickness. I think there will be other sick children and other sicknesses, and I wonder how Geishala will react to those. I hope Aud is past that superstition that Gieshala has. So this morning since Aud is back in her bed, Geishala seems happy. She even sings sweetly to Aud what sounds to me like a Viking lullaby, but I can't be certain. It is just the sound and rhythm of a lullaby that I recognize. It sounds like "Hush, Little Baby." but I'm not sure. Besides that is a song that my mom sang to me, and I sang to Audrey.

I decide to learn the Danish language as soon as possible as a safety measure, but not to let them know that I understand what they are saying.

While spinning, Geishala begins to cough. *Well, do we need to leave you out in a tree in the cold winter too? Are you a changeling?* I say nothing, but smile to myself. Instead of being cruel to Geishala, I find dried chickweed in the medicines, grind it into a powder, and make Geishala a tea with honey. Geishala seems to appreciate the gesture, but I can't be certain.

Chapter 9

All of a sudden, two young boys about twelve years old burst through the door of the room where I am spinning wool. The boys each have an axe in their hands. They rush to Geishala, and she gives them hugs and kisses. "Heidi, these are our two older sons, Ubba and Naddod. This is Heidi, your new governess and our new slave. Your father found her floating in the sea on a large piece of wood."

The boys look at me with mischief in their eyes. Ubba raises his axe as if to chop wood, but his blow is aimed at me. I step out of the way as his axe comes down on the table with a loud thud, and a piece chips out of the wooden table and flies off.

"No," Geishala screams and slaps him sharply across the cheek. "Floke is going to be angry at you, Ubba." I notice Ubba's flaming red hair that matches the color of Rollo's. Nothing about him looks like Floke or Geishala. "We are spinning. Go into the woods and find your father Floke and Rollo. Use your axes to help chop down trees not to chop up our furniture."

I feel glad that they are dismissed, but I wonder how Aud will ever survive in this environment. She notices that Geishala didn't ask the boys to put up their axes. This must be the reason Danish men are so fierce. They are raised to be without fear like these two children playing with axes, and none of the children seem to be sheltered or protected not even the baby. It is truly survival of the fittest. Again, I wonder how Danish children survive. It is surprising that they do.

Finally, the spinning is finished and Floke and Rollo come in to eat the midday meal of stew that has been simmering on the fire since last night. Ubba and Naddod come with them. "Since the boys are home, they will help peel the bark from the trees. Heidi can stay inside to help you, Geishala."

"Ah, good," Geishala says.

I am glad too. I want to stay near Aud in case her fever returns, and I don't care to work or even be around those two boys. I notice that Ubba and Naddod are quieter and calmer while Floke and Rollo are around. They might even be called sweet. I don't mind staying away from them. Even supervised, they frighten me like wild animals.

"Heidi will learn to make wool garments," Geishala says, coughing roughly.

"More chickweed tea?" I ask. "It will help your cough go away."

Without saying thank you, Geishala accepts the chickweed tea with wild honey. I notice that honey mead is the drink of choice for everyone during the midday meal. Kids drink honey mead too. I wonder of the effect it will have on Ubba and Naddod. Maybe they will mellow and not be so rough. The two boys seem to be around twelve years old. I think they are twins. Naddod has Floke's build, but Ubba is built like Rollo and favors Rollo. I look at Ubba and then at Rollo who winks at me.

"Come sit next to me," Rollo says to me.

"I will after I help Geishala bring the food in from the kitchen," I reply.

"She doesn't sit at the table with us. She is a slave," Ubba says, looking disapprovingly at me.

"She sits at the table if I say so," Rollo says and draws his hand to Ubba.

"Do not strike my son," Floke whispers in a deadly voice.

"Then I will eat in the kitchen with Heidi," Rollo replies. "I want to talk to her anyway."

I help Geishala bring the family's food to the long hall table, and the boys begin to eat at once. I feel the tension in the room, but I don't understand it. I am bothered by the lack of a prayer before the meal and their lack of table manners. I don't understand Rollo's insistence of going against Floke's wishes in Floke's house, but I don't understand their Danish ways.

Rollo and I make ourselves comfortable at the small table in the kitchen. I silently thank God for keeping me safe, saving me from drowning after the sinking of the *Titanic* and for my food and shelter. Rollo begins eating his meal and doesn't seem to notice my prayers. After we have finished eating, Rollo says, "Later this evening, I will begin training you to be a shield maiden. Those two boys will respect you more if you are a shield maiden and not just a slave."

I nod in agreement. There is no way I will survive the arrogance of Ubba and Naddod if I'm their slave. "I must help Geishala with her new garment because she isn't feeling well."

"I noticed that her color is pale," Rollo says.

Geishala comes through the door in time to hear Rollo's comment about her being pale. Suddenly her face turns blood red, making her look like a fiery blonde. "Time to go back to work," she says. She doesn't like that Rollo wanted to be alone with me. She sounds angry, and I don't understand why unless she is jealous. Something must have happened between her and Rollo.

I wasn't certain whether the anger was directed at Rollo or me. The Vikings are fierce and fiercely proud people. Weakness or sickness isn't tolerated. I notice that Geishala's anger caused her to begin coughing, but Rollo had quickly left the kitchen and was out the door of the long house. The boys and Floke went outside too. Geishala grabbed the chickweed powder and made herself more tea while I cleaned the table where the family had eaten. After the food was put away, the stew was set back on the oven to simmer for the rest of the day. Geishala says, "We must finish my cloak today. Then you may wear my old one." She motioned to it. "Wear it outside while you peel logs."

"Thank you," I say. "Are you feeling better?"

She does not answer me, but drinks more of her tea. We spin more wool and make part of a cloak until Rollo and Floke burst into the room. "We have felled enough trees to keep the boys busy for the rest of the afternoon. They were peeling bark with the spud. Rollo will begin training you, Heidi. Geishala, do you want to join us?"

"No," Geishala says. "I do not want to be a shield maiden. Actually, I have never wanted to sail or fight. Fighting is a man's job."

"Lots of Viking women are shield maidens and sail and fight," Floke says.

"Let's go," Rollo says. He has a glint in his eyes that I haven't seen before. Perhaps it is from chopping trees in the cold. Perhaps he is excited to be with me.

He goes into my sleeping room and returns with the shield and one of his large coats. "We will begin learning how to use these."

Hesitantly, Floke remains inside the long house with Geishala.

I put on the cloak that belongs to Rollo and hurry outside. The cloak is way too large for me, so Rollo places a wide leather belt around the middle, making it easier for me to move, but not much. I feel like a rodeo clown in his large coat, but it will be warm. I feel restricted like in a straight jacket from the tight belt. Then I think back to the tight clothing the English women on the *Titanic* wore. This was definitely better.

"If you can fight while wearing this cloak, you can fight well without it," Rollo says.

I wonder if I will still be here in the spring when he goes raiding. I desperately want to get back to 2022 and Audrey in America. I wonder if she is married yet. I remember the DNA results and my car accident. My toes still tingle. They don't feel normal yet. Sometimes at night, I wake unable to move and my mouth is so dry that my lips stick together. Since Ubba and Naddod came home, I am glad to learn how to defend myself here. I don't trust those two boys. Rollo shows me how to stand to hold the shield in front of me and to easily move it to the side. My arms soon began to ache from its weight. Rollo notices my fatigue and stops the physical training. Then he moves to teaching me to speak the Danish language. While looking at him standing so close to me, I notice that he has tatoos from his fingertips to his shoulders. I notice how manly he smells. I remember how long since my husband left. I remember missing him and feeling lonely.

Suddenly I hear Geishala call me from the kitchen, "Come here, Heidi. I don't feel well. Could you set out the food for us?"

I look at Rollo and enter the long hall and move on to the kitchen. I see that Geishala has a feverish red tint to her complexion and is acting sickly. Acting sickly isn't natural to these Danes. I rush to make her cornflower tea with honey. I realize that Geishala probably has the same sickness that Aud had. I figure it is a virus. I hope the rest of us don't catch it. *I wonder is she will be left out in the forest to die or be exchanged as Aud was. It would only be fair.*

I punch up the fire to heat the food, I add water to the stew so it won't burn and stir it with a ladle that I find on the rack, and then I set the heavy pot it on the long table in the long hall. Geishala retires to her bed. I realize that doing so was very difficult for her. Danish women can not show weakness in any way. No one comments, especially me.

"I will clean up after the meal," I tell her. "You rest." So beginning tonight, I do Geishala's day jobs of preparing food and tending to Aud. Of course, she has to give me directions because I am not familiar with their foods or recipes or cooking methods. I remember the chef on the *Titanic*. I hope he survived. He was excellent at his job. I wish I knew the names of who survived. When I get back to America, I will do some research. Finally, after a few days Geishala's cold or sickness is better. Geishala is able to come back to spinning, but she leaves the other work to me. I think she is wanting to keep me busy and close to her instead of outside with the men, especially Rollo. I wonder if she was really sick or whether Geishala was trying to prevent me from becoming a shield maiden and going on raiding trips with them. Then I remember that she actually had a fever, so I don't think that she was faking her sickness. I become determined to do both, so I start helping Ubba and Naddod peel bark from the logs in addition to taking care of Aud and preparing food. Cooking would have been easier in a more modern kitchen, but I manage. I pay more attention to Aud than her mother does anyway, and now that little girl seems very fond of me.

After all, a lot of American women from 2022 raise a family and work outside the home, but they do have modern conveniences and don't make all food from scratch. The work they do outside the home isn't usually physical.

I strap Aud onto my back by wrapping her with a band of cloth. It is much like the way Native American women strap their babies to their backs. Working so hard with a child strapped onto my back makes me get stronger more quickly. So if Geishala was planning to prevent me from becoming a shield maiden, it didn't work. I am beginning to love Aud as if she were my own child, and from what I can tell, she loves and trusts me. I wish she could go with me whenever we go raiding, but there is absolutely no way.

On the rainy days, I spin wool into yarn too. Soon there will be enough to make Geishala a new woolen cloak; but on the sunny days, I am back to helping Rollo and Floke peel logs. Rollo acts proud of my ability to work hard helping them while all the time having the baby strapped to my back. The Native American women did it all the time. Then I think of my DNA pie chart. I'm as much Native American as I am Danish if that chart is correct.

One night, Rollo comes to visit and have dinner at the long house. They call it sup. He says, "Floke, I want to buy Heidi. What is your price?"

Hearing him, Geishala says, "She is not for sale. She is our slave. We are keeping her. She will not become a shield maiden. She will not go to fight and raid with you."

Floke looks disturbed. "Geishala, come into the sleeping room. We need to discuss this. I am the master of my own house. This is my house. I am the master."

We hear the sounds of heated arguing. I haven't been fought over before.

While they are gone from the room, Rollo asks me to marry him. "I don't need a slave. What I need is a wife. Heidi, will you be my wife? They can not stop you from becoming my wife. They can stop you from becoming my slave. It is the Danish law."

When Floke and Geishala come back into the room, Rollo and I are locked in a romantic kiss because I said *yes*. All the time, I'm thinking that I'm not divorced. John and I never got divorced.

"I have changed my mind," Rollo says. "I am going to marry Heidi."

Taken by surprise, "There must be a period of courtship," Geishala explains. "You may wed her when the winter snow melts and the spring raids begin. Until then, she will be our slave. We will begin planning your wedding. You may wed before the spring raids begin. She will continue to train as a shield maiden and to help me at the same time. She is getting stronger. She takes such good care of Aud, although Ubba doesn't seem to like her."

So slowly and by degrees I get stronger and stronger every day. I have never worked so hard in my life. Suddenly the first flower of spring bursts through the snow. I am thrilled to see it. "It won't be long before we go raiding." Rollo toasts with honey mead at the evening meal. I will be able to carry my wife with me if I wish. You never wanted to go. Since the spring flowers have appeared, we will hunt for toads containing muscarin to eat before going to battle. They will make us fierce. Ubba and Naddod, you should help us to catch the toads. You might even get to go raiding with us if Geishala will let you."

The two boys look at their mother who looks distraught, but says nothing. Then they look at each other and beam because they know that they have won.

Then Rollo turns to me. I was beginning to catch on to some of their language, and I heard what he said about Geishala never wanting to go, but I said nothing. I had been acting as if I didn't understand the Danish language so they would talk more freely around me. "Tomorrow we will take the old ship that is moored in the bay and sink it."

"Sink it?" I ask. "Floke, are you going to let Rollo sink your ship?"

"It is how we get rid of the rats," Ubba says. "Are you afraid of rats, slave?"

"No. I am not," I say. I feel that Geishala's dislike of me had transferred to Ubba. I thought about it. I didn't really care for Ubba either. Perhaps it was just a dislike of all slaves in general. I thought about Audrey in America. I hope I didn't ever treat anyone as badly as Ubba treats me. This was worse than the classes on the *Titanic*. Being a Danish person's slave was much worse than being lower class in England.

"Ah, Mama, there is a witch girl in the village," Ubba says. "She wants me to bring our slave girl to see her."

"No, she has no time to go," Geishala says. "She has much work to do here."

I was pleased to hear this because I didn't want to go anywhere with Ubba.

"Then may I bring the witch girl to our house to see our slave girl? She is a seer. She can see the future. I would like to know what the witch girl thinks of our slave girl that Floke found floating in the sea. Who knows? Our slave girl may be a witch too."

"Let him bring her," Rollo says. "I would like to know what the outcome of our raids in the spring will be. If she is a true seer, maybe she can tell us."

That night, I dream that I'm a witch in Salem, Massachusetts. I dream I am tied out in the square for all to see. I am a convicted witch and scheduled to hang the next day although the American movies had the witches burned at the stake.

But the next day, Ubba walks into the long room with a strange looking slave girl. She is dressed in rags, and her hair is matted and dirty. She is covered with filth and smells bad. He has her tied to his waist by a cord. "If she gets away, I am in trouble with her owner, Valer" he says. "He said he would cut my nuts off." Rollo and Floke laugh at this.

I do not like her appearance and mostly, I don't believe in seers.

"You should have left her in the village," Geishala says. "We don't want her here. She smells bad."

Ubba rolls his eyes and starts to usher her back out the door.

"No, no, no," Rollo exclaims. "Wait! I want to know the outcome of our spring raids. Can you tell me that, witch girl?"

With gleaming green eyes focused only on Rollo, the witch girl says, "You will be captured and forced to be baptized a Christian. You will need a Trojan horse."

Chapter 10

"A Christian?" Rollo asked the witch girl although he already knew. "What is that?"

"Christians have one god and do not believe in Odin or Thor."

"I am a Christian," I say. I knew he already knew, but I had to answer.

"Leif Erickson is a Christian," Floke says.

Everyone in the room turns to glare at me as if I had said I was from outer space, except Danes don't know about outer space. At least I didn't think these Danish folks knew about outer space. I had read that Leif Erickson was baptized a Christian.

"Heidi, come to the kitchen to talk to me about our wedding," Rollo asks.

Once we were securely away from the others, Rollo says, "Please don't say that aloud. Don't say that you are a Christian. Ubba and Naddod are ignorant, arrogant and might try to harm you. Floke and Geishala are not Christian. I truly don't care that you are Christian, but in their ignorance, they will take offense." Then he kissed me on the lips. "We need to get married as soon as possible, so that those two won't be tempted to harm you.

They wouldn't dare harm my wife. They are afraid of me and if they aren't, they should be. After all, you are their slave girl, and they are raging bucks with raging hormones.

When we entered the main room again, Ubba had taken the witch girl back to the village and her owner. Her stench remained in the room. Rollo announced very loudly, "I can't wait to marry this woman. Heidi will become my bride tomorrow, and we will sail tomorrow."

"No, she can not," Geishala objects. The look on Geishala's face was of pure pain.

Floke looked at her with a questioning look. "It will take a few days longer to get all the ships ready."

"We aren't prepared. Her dress is not ready." Geishala explains, trying to keep Floke from being angry.

"No problem," Rollo says. "I will bring her one from the village tonight. We will marry in two days then. She will be my wife. I don't know what a Trojan horse is, but if I am captured, I want this woman by my side. She will teach me what a Trojan horse is and what it does. Geishala, I will pay for her with silver that I got on our last raid. I want Heidi to go raiding with us as soon as possible, but I think we will raid in France instead of Mercia. Floke, can I purchase that ship that you were trying out when you found Heidi? It is already ready to go?"

"You are going raiding in France with only one ship?"

"Yes, raiding France will be easy," Rollo replied. "I may ask Leif Erickson to join us or we will join him. He has a fleet of ships. His ships are always ready because raiding and transport is his business. Come to think of it, it is mine too now."

"Toast to our raid next week," he raises his horn of honey mead. They raise their horns too. Everyone is in a happy mood except Geishala. She excuses herself and leaves the room. She says she has something to do.

"We must go out and begin caulking the cracks in that ship. It will need to be scraped and caulked with wool. Heidi, can you help me? We will stuff some wool strips into the cracks and then wet the wool. When it is wet, it will swell and make the ship waterproof."

"Will Stiff Beard be going with you?" Floke asks.

"No, Ragnar won't be going this time," Rollo replies. "Feydis his wife won't let him." Rollo laughs heartily. "We don't need him. I can't wait to see the look on his ugly face when we come back with our ship full of treasure. Or yours either, my friend."

"Geishala, could you sell us some strips of wool to caulk the cracks between the boards in our ship?" Rollo yells toward the room Geishala retired to.

"Sure." She angrily stalks backs into the room and walks over to the spinning wheel and grabs a sack of raw wool and thrusts it toward Rollo. "This will cost you, Rollo the Difficult, for taking my slave, but I want jewels. Not silver. I will take silver now, but you must bring me jewels back when you go raiding in France. I want elegant French jewels, and I want silver, too. Heidi will cost you a fortune, you idiot."

Rollo takes the bag of wool from Geishala, and he and I go outside to caulk his ship. I guess it is my ship too since I am to be his wife, but I don't really understand the laws governing Danes. Probably, I have no rights to own property. From what Floke said to Geishala, everything belongs to the man of the house. It isn't joint ownership.

Caulking the ship is harder than it sounds. Sinking the ship had removed the rats and fleas. I was proud of that, but shoving and hammering the wool strips into the cracks between the boards of the bottom of the ship is very difficult. We use a knife and a hammer. If you didn't hold the knife just so, it cuts through the wool, rendering it unusable. But making certain the ship is waterproof is important. Whatever Rollo was doing, they wanted to do. I think that they idolized Rollo and only tolerated me because he liked me because they were only civilized to me when he was nearby. Actually, they frightened me and like dogs or wild animals, they probably sensed my fear. They could smell it.

I realized that I had left Aud inside with Geishala, so I excused myself to go check on her. I was certain that I could stuff cracks with her strapped to my back. I knew she was safer with me than she was inside in her crib alone because Geishala often ignored her cries for long periods of time. Geishala reminded me of a drug addicted mother who slept all the time, but it was just her way. She wouldn't win "Mother of the Year." I wondered what would happen to the baby whenever I married Rollo. I felt sad that I must leave Aud behind with her mother, Ubba, and Naddod. Again, I thought of Audrey in America. When I left her, she was graduating from college. I wish we were going raiding to America instead of France or Mercia, but Native Americans were all we would find there now, and they didn't have any gold or silver. Those metals didn't concern them. Their primary concern was surviving. It was not getting rich. They traded beads and shells.

Once inside the long house, I take Aud from her crib and wrap her securely in a long piece of fabric and strap her to my back, knotting the fabric under her butt. Aud has been close to me in this wrapped manner for so many days now that she seems to like it. I like it too. I take her back outside tied on my back to hammer more wool into the cracks in the ship. Putting my trust in strips of wool in the rough seas is a very frightening thought, especially since I almost drowned from the sinking of the *Titanic*, and it had been made of steel. I had known the *Titanic* was going to sink, but I don't have the same information about this Viking raid.

I think about the DNA results and my car accident. I remember being pronounced DOA at the hospital. It is a miracle that I am here. I never felt dead. As if I knew what being dead felt like. Everything has worked out as if I dreamed the entire trip on the *Titanic*, and it came true. I'm actually getting married tomorrow to Rollo, a Danish man. At home in America with Audrey, I never even dated another man after her father left us. No one ever seemed good enough for Audrey Lodbrok. No one could replace John Lodbrok. Not for me and not for Audrey, but he is gone, and I'm not even home. John Lodbrok could have been of Danish descent. He probably was. Now, I was getting married to another Danish man named Lodbrok, and I love him and this changeling baby that we saved from the fairies and perhaps even from the wolves and bobcats. The baby's name was also Aud. Aud and Audrey. Quite a coincidence. I wondered if Rollo would ever meet Audrey. I didn't think that was possible, considering the time difference. I needed to figure out how to travel in time back to America. I wondered if I married Rollo whether I would miss him like I missed my husband after he left.

I rejoined Rollo on the ship. He looked up and smiled. "Ah, Heidi. Are you taking Aud with us to France? Raiding is no place for a baby. Raiding is dangerous. It is too dangerous even for these young bucks. He motioned toward Ubba and Naddod. "I know you are going to miss Aud, but she will be here when we return."

"I know, but I'm going to miss her. I worry about her."

"We leave tomorrow as soon as we are married. We need to catch the tide. I am so excited."

"Excited to marry me or excited to go raiding in France?"

"Both. You wench. I won't sleep any tonight, but I have to go to the village to get you a wedding dress. Remember, I promised Geishala that I would. I also want to invite Leif Erickson to join us on our raid. By the way, what is a Trojan horse?"

"Trojan horse? It is a way to get inside a place without anyone suspecting what you are doing."

"That is exactly what we need, a Trojan horse."

Chapter 11

The next morning Rollo slips into my bedroom before I get up, but he doesn't wake me. I've been awake for hours. I have so much on my mind. Alhtough I am ready to leave here, I am concerned for Aud. First, I'm concerned what Audrey will think about me marrying a Danish man who will be dead long before she is born. Then, I'm concerned for baby Aud. Although she isn't my baby, but both Rollo and I love her. She is not a changeling. He proved that with the clothing change. Neither he nor I believe in changelings. Then I think about the Viking raids. I am excited about them, but I know that they will be dangerous.

Rollo throws a package onto the bed. "Try it on. It is your wedding dress," he says.

"I will, but you can't see me in it before our wedding. It is bad luck."

"I didn't think that you were superstitious. I don't need any bad luck."

"It is just a tradition. I am a little superstitious. Don't you want our raids to be successful?"

"Yes, I do," he replies and exits the room to the long hall. "I will wait for you. We need to get married as soon as possible so we can load onto the ships and head out."

"Ships? So Leif Erickson is joining us?"

"We are actually joining him. We are sailing west toward your America."

"Oh, Rollo," I threw the furs back and bounded toward the fire in the main room. I am more excited to be going to America than I ever imagined. I wondered how Rollo would fit in my America of 2022. I wondered what year it would be in my America. Would it be 2022? Would Audrey be there? Would the sailing on these Viking ships be smoother and safer than the *Titanic* had been? How long would it take us? I begin grabbing things that I thought I'd need on the ship and for when we reached America. I make a pouch of bindweed, a purgative; toadflax for ulcers; marsh marigold, to keep elves from milk pails; chickweed, for coughs; and cornflower, for fevers. I find all these in Gieshala's stash. My pouch is equivalent to a trip to Wal-Mart before a vacationing trip in America. Then I head to the kitchen to see what food Geishala might let me have and to see Aud.

"Good morning, Geishala," I say. "As soon as we are packed, will you help me into my wedding dress? We are getting married early this morning and sailing as soon as possible."

"I know. Ubba and Naddod are as excited as you are, or maybe more so, but they aren't happy that you are going. I'm not either."

"I didn't know they were going," I reply, trying to keep my voice steady and not let Geishala know that I am disappointed. Truthfully, Ubba frightens me and Naddod does everything he suggests. Naddod is Ubba's shadow. I am not happy to hear this news. I hoped they are not to be on the ship with me, but I bet they are because it is Rollo's. If so, I won't be able to relax. I thought about it. I'm certain that this sailing trip will be anything but relaxing no matter who is on the ship. Compared to the *Titanic*, the Viking ship is tiny and fragile. It is powered by one large sail for wind and by oars. There is no way to get out of the elements. It is designed for short trips. I'm certain it will take us at least a month to reach America. I was apprehensive before I found out that those two boys are going along. Now, I'm sick to my stomach.

"I wish you would come with us, Geishala," I say. Actually, I'm not certain how America would like her, but I didn't mention that. I thought of the "old money" women on the *Titanic* and Geishala. "Rollo says we are sailing with Leif Erickson to America. You would love America."

"I can't," she replies. "You just don't understand. I must stay here with Floke. He has many more ships to build. He is my husband."

I consider this to mean that she loves Floke.

"Could we get some food to carry with us?"

"Rollo brought some from the village. He has already packed it on your ship. This is not his first voyage. You are not his first wife."

I felt as if she had slapped me. I realize that Geishala doesn't want to be my friend, not now or ever. So I walk to where Aud is eating her breakfast. I can't say that I am not glad to be away from Geishala. I grab Aud to my chest and hug her tightly. I know in my heart that this is the last day that I'd ever see her. I think about my Audrey and wonder if I will ever see her again either. She visited my dreams at night, but in my dreams she couldn't understand what I was saying to her. My heart hurts with missing Audrey. No matter what, I must get back to her. I feel the tingling in my toes that started during the automobile accident in England. It reminds me that I am alive, but lost somewhere in the world in another time. I desperately want to get back to America 2022.

"Rollo can help you into that dress," Geishala said. "Then he will be eager to help you get out of it." She took Aud from me, and wrapped her in her cloak. Then she hurried outside. "I have much to do for Ubba and Naddod, and I want to see Leif Erickson." I notice how she always said Ubba's name first. He is her favorite son. Or maybe he is the older twin.

I look around the empty kitchen and know in my heart that I won't be returning here and that I won't see baby Aud ever again. I will miss Aud. That is all. I would not miss Geishala.

Suddenly, Rollo bursts through the door with another man that I don't recognize. He is dressed in a long dark cloak and has a Santa beard and braids. "Magus is marrying us. Get that wedding dress on, Heidi. We need to leave with the tide. We must hurry. If we miss the tide, the men will be exhausted from rowing on the first day, and they won't ever get rested. Tired raiders are bad luck."

I look at him. Then I rush to the other room to put on the wedding dress. There seems to be no one except him to help me with my dress. I feel doomed from the start, remembering how bad luck it is for him to see me before our ceremony such that it will be. We have no attendants, no flowers, and no witnesses.

"I guess that you will have to help me," I say from the other room. I feel his presence and turn to face him.

His eyes gleam. "I'm right behind you."

The dress is beautiful and I'm amazed at the intricate work on it. It overlaps and laces down the back with a leather ribbon or strip, so it is one size or one size fits most. Of course, there aren't any sizing tags. It is a beautiful, soft, white deer leather. I strip to my underwear, and Rollo helps me into the dress. "Your skin is so soft," he says. "It reminds me of silks from the Mediterranean."

"You have been to the Mediterranean? I would like to go there."

"We are going to America first. Leif says that America is inhabited by savages."

"They are called Indians." I answer. "According to American history, Leif discovers America before Christopher Columbus, but whenever Columbus discovered America, he thought it was the Indies. He named the savages Indians, but really they are Native Americans. Really, America belongs to them and it always has. I am part Native American.

"Who is this Christopher Columbus? You are a witch, my love. Did you bewitch him too?"

"I will tell you when we get on the ship. Okay? And I am not a witch. I've lived in America before. Actually Columbus comes to America after Leif Erickson."

"Okay. Let's get married and go to America. Let me lace up the back of that beautiful dress, but it is not as beautiful as you are. I brought you a shield maiden outfit and some metal wrist bands too. Have you learned to braid your hair yet? Our hair will need to be braided while on the ship because of the wind and the sun. The wind and elements will tangle and whip it to a crisp hay texture. There won't be any fresh water to waste on bathing and cleaning our hair. All fresh water must be carried with us, and it is for drinking only. If your hair is braided, it is much easier to keep the wind from tangling it. On our ship, we don't have an area below deck, so we will be exposed day and night to wind, rain, and sun. Finally, Rollo finishes lacing me into my wedding dress. I am so excited. I think I am more excited today than I was the day that I boarded the airplane to come to England. That was the same day of my car accident.

The little man that Rollo had brought with him to marry us says, "Stand here and join hands. With Odin's blessings, you two are married. May the gods be with you." There were no people present. There were no witnesses except that little man. Suddenly, Rollo wraps me in a tight, romantic embrace. How can this marriage be real? There are only three people here, but it doesn't matter because legally I'm still married to John Lodbrok.

"My wife, my shield maiden, my witch," Rollo says. "Now, let's get you dressed in your shield maiden clothes. It is time for us to depart. I would like to linger and enjoy the view of my beautiful wife, but the tide is calling. I will enjoy you on the ship."

"I want to say good-bye to Floke and Geishala. They have been good to me. And Aud. I don't want to leave her."

"We will be back, my darling. We aren't staying in America forever."

Somehow, I had the feeling that I was. I was staying in America forever. If I ever got back to America, I didn't think I would ever want to leave. If I ever got back to America, it would be my quest to find Audrey.

I just hope to reach it safely, but somehow I don't think that would ever happen. The seas and storms are rough. I hope we are traveling south of all icebergs.

I remove my beautiful wedding dress and dress in the shield maiden clothing that Rollo has purchased for me: leather pants, a lace-up-the-front linen tunic, a leather vest, and tons of metal arm bands. There are no Danish wedding rings. I take my shield and my sword from the wall. I lace the tall leather shield maiden boots. These clothes are for protection from the elements and for protection while fighting. Secretly, I hope that there will be no fighting, but I am certain that if we make it to America alive, the savages will fight us to protect their land. I really don't blame them. In my heart, I know that we will encounter savages. I wonder how these leather clothes will feel after they get wet from the spray of the waves. I guess they will dry in the sun. I remember the phrase "rode hard and put up wet."

Taking the bag of herbs that I packed in case of medical emergencies, and my wedding dress, we rush outside to board the ship at the landing. As I grab the dress, I remember the silk dress that Margaret Brown gave me on the *Titanic*. The oarsmen have already placed their shields in the holders along the sides of the ship above the oars. These hand-crafted ships are something to behold. I haven't seen many ships since the one that Floke sailed when I was rescued, except the one that we sunk to remove the rats and fleas. I didn't know which one this was, but the hand carvings were spectacular. Each one had a dragon head in the front. Leif Erickson's ships are gigantic next to Rollo's. I remember that his father is Eric the Red. Someone there must have plenty of money because sailing is their business.

I look at the fleet and at Floke. I nod to him and smile. I give him a small wave. He had built all these ships by hand. He really is a master craftsman, and he seems to be a kind man. At least, he has always been kind to me. I look around for Geishala. She stands there straightening her sons' clothing and giving instructions like any nervous mother.

I walk over to where they stand. "I will watch out for them," I say to her. It is the least I can do.

"Ha. And who will watch out for you?" She turns and walks away.

I suppose that I need to leave her alone, but I follow her. "Geishala, why do you hate me so much?"

"Who do you think Rollo's first wife was? You are so stupid."

"Who? He hasn't told me."

"Ask him." Again, she walks further away.

I stand there in shock. She had been married to Rollo? Surely not. But it would make sense the way she acts.

"Time to board the ship." Suddenly a chant in unison rises from the oarsmen.

"Ump. Ump. Ump. Ump," they chant. They pound on their shields with their fists. That has to hurt. I think.

I want to talk to Geishala more about her declaration, but I must get on the ship. I stride across the pier and step onto the ship. A strange feeling passes over me. I am as frightened to board this ship as I was to board the *Titanic*. My heart races and sweat pops up on my face even in this cold temperature. I guess it is PTSD. I take a deep breath. I think about history and relax somewhat, but even in this cold temperature, sweat beads on my forehead. I know that Leif Erickson makes it to

America, but there is no recording of whether he and his ships arrive in one piece of not, and there is no mention of Rollo. I look at the size of Erickson's Viking ship and the size of Rollo's. I remember Rollo's is designed to be able to sail into rivers and streams when raiding. And according to the *Titanic*, bigger isn't always better. I look around at our crew. Ubba and Naddod are not among the men who are our oarsmen. There is no place on our ship for them to hide. For that I am thankful. I'm certain Rollo had something to say about that. I truly hope that they are already on one of the other ships, maybe Leif Erickson's ship. I might relax a little if they are. Ubba frightens me as much as anyone here.

We catch the outgoing tide. With the tide and our sails, the men don't have to row.

So for the next day and night, everything goes well. Then one of the oarsmen sees a raven fly toward the ship. Ravens mean death to the Vikings.

"No, No, No," he yells. "Shoo bird!" Rollo joins in the racket trying to shoo the bird, but in spite of their hand waving and yelling, the raven comes to land on the mast.

"You are the most superstitious people I've ever seen. It is just a bird, a raven," I tell Rollo.

"Who didn't want me to see her in her wedding dress before the wedding? A raven means death and bad luck. The gods say so," Rollo says. "You are superstitious too."

"Okay. Change the subject," I answer. "Tell me about Leif Erickson."

"His father is Eric the Red. His family is in the business of sailing and trading merchandise with other countries, but he was banished from Norway. Leif was born in Greenland. Eric served King Olaf I Tryggvason and was converted to Christianity. Olaf wants Eric to spread Christianity to other lands."

"Is he your friend?"

"Yes, I guess you would say so."

"In America, there is a holiday named Leif Erickson Day. It is October 9."

"Perhaps when we reach America, there will be a Rollo Lodbrok Day? Huh?"

"Perhaps," I reply, but I know that there isn't. Our ship doesn't have a compartment below deck, so our belongings and us are exposed to the elements all day and night. The nights are freezing cold so I wrap in excess sail material that I found folded and laying on the deck, and the days are scorching hot. All this is bearable except the rain. Day or night, torrential rain is like getting beaten. One minute we are close to the other ships, and then the next we are far apart on the sea, and they are barely visible on the horizon. I like it better whenever they are close to us because their presence is comforting, but we are wind-powered and man-powered. I can't help but worry about icebergs. I scan the water, but I never see any. Perhaps we are south of the icebergs. I hope so.

After a few weeks of days and nights of extreme temperatures, a tremendous storm with high winds attacks us during the night. On the ship, time is hard to figure except night and day. I wonder if it is a tornado like I've seen on radar on the Weather Channel. I know tornados often start out in the ocean. We are blown off course and far away from Leif's ships. I am so frightened. The waves wash over the sides of the ship. Everyone is drenched. My leather clothing feels heavy from the water.

During the night, one oarsman is washed overboard from our ship. His brother doesn't know what to do with himself since he is gone. I feel sorry for him. I really don't blame him for grieving. He misses his brother. There are often has tears in his eyes. Of the two of them, I liked the second man better. He is called Bein.

I have the feeling that theses Danes don't like me. I am an outsider to them. Traveling through time, makes me an outsider to most people. I don't even understand it myself. I remember my time on the *Titanic*. No one believed me whenever I told them that the ship was going to sink, especially Captain Smith. Perhaps these Danes think that I'm a witch too. Or they don't think I should be married to Rollo because they don't really know me. Bein never said anything derogatory to me, but went along with his brother while he was on board. They seemed to prefer that I wasn't around, so I found me a corner in the front of the ship to ride. I remember the sinking of the *Titanic* and floating in the ocean for so long holding on to that piece of wooden furniture. I remember the terrified feeling I had until I passed out. The situation was more than my system could handle.

I look around for something to use as a floatation device on this ship, but I see nothing. I should have thought about this earlier. I should have been more concerned with safety than with a wedding. Maybe I can use my wooden shield to float if I need it. I feel afraid. My heart is beating so loudly that I hear it. I think others can hear it too. My being afraid may be why the crew doesn't like me. The waves get higher with each gust of wind and roll over the sides of our ship. The water is extremely cold. Still, I don't see any icebergs. I haven't mentioned icebergs to the crew or to Rollo. I clutch the sides of our ship as do the others to keep from getting washed overboard. Suddenly, a huge wave comes crashing on board, and one entire row of the oarsmen is swept overboard. With nothing to help them float, they perish below the waves. I wonder why they aren't holding to their shields. I think the shields would float. Perhaps it would be bad luck to use them except during fighting a battle. In that case, superstition should take a backseat. If it was me, I would use them to prevent sinking maybe prevent drowning.

With another burst of wind and water, our mast cracks, and the sail comes crashing down. One man is killed whenever the large wooden pole pins him to the deck. I'm covered with the fabric from the sail to help keep myself dry, but I grab onto one piece of the cracked mast. It will float. I untangle myself from the sail slowly and with difficulty because the wet sail clings to me, the ship is rocking, and the wind is horrible. The wind is blowing hard and in violent gusts. It blows cold, salty water onto the ship. There isn't much to hold on to except the sides of the ship where those men who were rowing were swept overboard. With the next huge blast of waves, Rollo and I are swept overboard. I hear my own screams. I have a feeling like I've done this before. We land in the sea and are sinking fast. Rollo is holding my hand, but the force of the water makes him turn loose. I am sinking fast and don't know what happened to him. It reminds me of sinking off the *Titanic*, except this ship is floating in pieces not sinking intact. I feel my body sinking deeper into the sea. I can't breathe. Water seems to fill my lungs, cutting off my oxygen. I am clutching a piece of the wooden mast. Suddenly, I float to the surface with the help of that wood. The wood of the mast is buoyant like that wooden piece of furniture was floating when the *Titanic* sunk. The winds have settled somewhat, but the waves are carrying me away from the ship. Whenever they carry me near the shore, I kick my feet with any strength I can find and paddle toward the white sand on the beach. I wonder what beach this is. I hope it is North America. We had been sailing for days, so maybe it is. The waves calm somewhat, and I am transported toward shore by the natural movement of the waves. Soon the beach becomes littered with the bodies of Danish men and pieces of Rollo's precious Viking ship. Finally, I can stand, but then another huge wave knocks me down. I get tons of sand inside my leather shield maiden suit. It feels like wearing sandpaper.

Soon, I am deposited on the wet sand of the beach by the waves. I think I'm unconscious. I taste salty sea water. If I was unconscious, I couldn't taste, could I. It reminds me of how my mouth tasted after the sinking of the *Titanic*. I look out toward the sea and see Leif Erickson's ship on the horizon. As far as I can tell from here, it is in one piece, not broken by the strong waves like Rollo's. I think about Ubba and Naddod. They are safe. Somehow Leif's ships are spared by the storm and I am too. Being snatched from death is becoming a theme or story of my life. I hear the Vikings sounding their horn, so any survivors will know that help is near. I hear Rollo calling my name, but I can't answer. I don't think that I'm unconscious. I have swallowed so much water. I think that I survived the sinking of the *Titanic*, and I've survived a Viking shipwreck. I hope I'm back in America. I am alive. I want to answer Rollo, but he seems so far away. I'm back where I wanted to be. I must find Audrey, and America is where she lives. This is why I boarded the *Titanic* knowing that it was going to sink. I wonder what year this is. I hope it is 2022, but I look at the shore and the beach. There is no sign of modernization. Finally, Rollo finds me.

"Heidi, are you alive?" he asks, shaking me. "We must get to Leif Erickson's ship. We must return to Vinland."

I try to answer. I can not. I don't want to return to Vinland. I want to be here is America. I love Rollo, but I desperately want to stay in America. I want to find Audrey and 2022.

Rollo thinks that I'm dead. "I need to bury her," I hear him say. Leif Erickson's horn sounds again, but this time it is a different message. I don't understand the messages, but I think it is Rollo's message to return to the ship if he is alive. My eyes are slightly open. Rollo waves his arms to signal that he is alive. He has to leave me and swim to Leif Erickson's rescue canoe. If he stays another second, they may think that he is dead too. They may leave without him.

I can not move or speak. I want to stay here. I think. So I act like I'm dead.

"Ah, Heidi, I must go. The savages are near. You called them Indians or Native Americans. You said that they own this land."

Now, I hear their whoops. I am not really afraid of them. I remember my DNA results. I am part Native American, and apparently, I am difficult to kill.

"I want to bury your body, but there is no time. I must go to Erickson's ship before he leaves me. I love you. I will return here to find you in another time and another place."

Rollo touches my cheek. I hope he can not tell by the warmth of my cheek that I'm alive, but I've been floating in the water so long that my cheek feels cold. I feel cold. There is no blood in my face. "You are gone, my darling wife. I never got the chance to tell you. Geishala hates you because she was my first wife. She is jealous of you."

Suddenly, the horn on Erickson's ship sounds again louder and closer to the shore, and they lower a canoe over the side to come to pick up Rollo. He leaves me. He thinks I am dead. I think that is better for him, so he won't blame himself for leaving me or try to come back to rescue me.

I'm glad he didn't bury me because again I'm not dead. Again, I hear the whoops of the Native Americans. I wonder why people think I'm dead whenever I'm not. I wonder why my dreams are filled with hospital beds and dreams and smells of sickness and death.

Audrey

Our plane with my mother, my friend Julian the registered nurse, and me lands in Memphis. Then my mother is loaded into an ambulance and carried to the Baptist Hospital. Still, she is unconscious.

Once she is settled in the ICU, my father comes to visit her. Neither of us can visit often because of Covid protocol. We must be tested, washed, and suited.

"Mom, you are home now. Please wake up," I ask.
She doesn't.

Chapter 12

At once, Rollo is gone and the whoops of the Native Americans come closer and louder. They are on the beach with me. Again, I try to move, make a sound, or at least open my eyes. I can only open my eyes a small slit. I am exhausted from being on the ship in the elements and being washed overboard, but I am not dead. Rollo has left me on the beach, but I am not in 2022 where I need to be. I think of the Native American portion of my ancestry DNA chart. I open my eyes wider. I hope I don't get scalped. I wonder where exactly I am on the coast of North America. I wonder which Indian tribe these are. I've studied the Indians of North America. From the way they are dressed, I think these are probably the Powhatan which would make this coastal Virginia, but I can't be certain until I see their houses. I will know if I see their bark wigwams. The Powhatan are semi- nomadic and move seasonally to follow the game that provides their food, clothing, and shelter. They live in tents made of skins or wigwams fashioned with four saplings bent toward the center and covered with strips of bark sewn together. They use bark from hickory, walnut, locust, and hornbeam trees. I can identify those barks.

Swamp grass provides a lining to keep out the cold and to absorb leaks. I think of stuffing the strips of wool into the cracks in the hull of the ship. These people use the natural resources to survive. The door opening is covered with animal skins, and a fire is built in the center of the hut. Hopefully, the smoke escapes through the door.

If they take me prisoner, maybe I will at least get fed. I feel the hunger in my belly and the tingling in my toes. My toes have tingled since my automobile crash in England or maybe from floating in the frigid ocean. I don't remember exactly when they started. I wonder if it would be safer for me to act dead or for me to open my eyes and try to speak and move. I am eager to see their wigwams. I want to know what kind of Native Americans these are, but most of all, I don't want to be scalped or worse.

Finally, two Indian men come near me. They are wearing moose hides. It is still cold here in North America. One of them indicates to the other that I'm alive and female. The other starts to take my scalp and is stopped by the first. "Her hair is yellow." He says.

"Yellow hair?" The first seems fascinated. He picks me up and throws me onto his back over his shoulder. I slip into unconsciousness again. I seem to have cheated death again. When I wake, I touch my head. I still have my hair, and I am still alive and so far, unharmed. I wonder if I'm dreaming that I'm alive or if I really am. My dreams have been filled with near death situations recently. I glance around me. I see Powhatan women tanning hides. They are dipping their hands in pots of brains and rubbing it onto the hides. They are chattering to each other, probably about me I think because they glance my way ever so often. I see children running around in the camp. All the wigwams are close together. Over to one side I see what I figure to be a sweathouse. Steam escapes from the door covering like smoke escapes from their door openings. I look beyond to their wigwams built near each other. They look much like I thought they would. These people are Powhatan. I'm in Virginia. That is good. They are not the most aggressive tribe that I've studied. Perhaps they will let me live with them until I figure out how to get back to 2022 and Audrey.

I see the shaman's quocosin over to one side of the group of wigwams. Maybe the shaman knows how to be transported through time. After being fed smoked fish, I am carried to the wigwam to sweat. It is probably a good idea because travelers from other regions are who helped to thin out the Native Americans by bringing them diseases. Although some of the diseases were transmitted through sex, some were not, like small pox. I realize that sweating is one of their methods like medicine to remove impurities from the body. They are protecting themselves from me, and I know the sweat will remove the Viking's toxins from my body if there are any and of course, there are. I wonder what Rollo is doing now. I wonder about Audrey. I wonder if either of them miss me. The only person I know will be glad that I'm gone is Geishala except that I was a useful slave. Then I remember Rollo telling me that she was his first wife.

The Native Americans drag me into the sweat lodge, and tell me to sit next to a particular woman. We sit around a fire in the sweat lodge. Someone is designated to feed the fire, but not just keep it going. They are to build it up to a roaring blaze that raises the temperature in the lodge to make us sweat. They do a great job. I begin to sweat and the more I sweat, the better I feel. I am amazed. Then I am dragged from the wigwam and thrown into the snow. Snow is rubbed along my limbs and my torso. Now, I am to do it for myself. It closes the pores, and it feels wonderful. I am still wearing the wet leather shield maiden clothes that Rollo bought me. I notice that they are discussing my clothing.

After the snow rub, I'm dragged to a wigwam on this end of the village and shoved inside through the hide opening doorway. Several people live in this wigwam together. I look around.

I see several pallets for sleeping scattered around on the mats on the floor. Several other women and children will sleep here too. A woman points to my pallet. I've been provided with a moose skin for a blanket. I say, "Thank you." I nod and smile.

She snorts. She is one of the people who was talking about my shield maiden clothing.

I don't think that she is happy to see me. I don't know if I am a slave here or not, but I figure that I am. I have gone from being a slave, to being a wife, and back to being a slave in a matter of a few days. I am so exhausted that I fall onto my pallet. I cover myself with the moose hide and remove my wet leather boots and pants. I've had these wet pants and boots on so long that I'm certain I'll have a yeast infection. It is like wearing a wet bathing suit for too long. Taking off the wet, leather clothing feels good too. I hope they dry while laying near the fire. It will take me some getting used to the smokiness of the wigwam because there is only a small opening for the smoke to escape. It reminds me of the Vikings long house, but it isn't as big. I think about lung cancer. I notice that the floor of the wigwam is several mats of cattails woven together. I think about the jobs that these Indian women do daily. I wonder if I will be taught to tan hides or sew leather clothing. I could be put in charge of tending children. I hope I will be tending little children, but sometimes children can be cruel.

The near drowning in the sea and the sitting for hours in the sweat lodge have taken all my energy. Quickly, I fall asleep and fall into dreams of people standing around me in a hospital bed. In my dream, Audrey is singing me a song in a very soft, low voice.

Suddenly, I feel someone slide under the moose hide next to me. I am frightened, but soon I realize that it is a small Indian girl child who is looking for warmth. In the morning, the others in the hut will see that the child isn't frightened of me. I am surprised myself, but I am glad. Maybe they will not be frightened either.

The others wake at sunrise and see that the little girl is still snuggled next to me. I reach for my shield maiden outfit, but find that it is gone. I wrap the moose hide around myself to cover my nakedness, although I'm still wearing my underwear and the linen shirt that I arrived here wearing. "Where are my clothes?" I ask one of the women, the one who snorted at me last night. She shoves a moose hide jacket or coat toward me. I hold it up to my shoulders. It nearly reaches the floor. The jacket is beautiful and decorated with tiny sea shells. I wonder if it belonged to the woman who is handing it to me. I examine it and discover that it is also decorated with porcupine quills. There is a belt to keep the jacket closed. She gives me a pair of moccasins. I am honored, but I still want my shield maiden clothes. I didn't make it ashore with my beautiful leather wedding dress that Rollo Lodbrok had bought me, so I felt especially attached to my leather shield maiden clothes, but I don't know how to ask for them. And I don't know where they are.

Again in English, I ask, "Where are my clothes?"

She doesn't answer, but snorts at me again. I dress in the clothing and moccasins that she has handed me. "One more language to learn," I say. I smile and say, "Thank you." I look around the inside of the wigwam. It is made by four saplings bent toward the center and covered with bark strips sewn together with stripes of deer hide. The inside is covered with what looks like swamp grass to keep out the water. I hope it works.

My benefactor notices me looking at the walls of the wigwam and says, "*Here* in her language which I think is Algonquan." She hands me a piece of smoked fish and some nuts to eat for breakfast. I have arrived in the winter and for her to share their food with me is remarkable.

"Thank you," I say again and smile. The food is delicious and fresh.

She may be easier to win over than Gieshala was. I keep smiling at her. Then I remember Rollo saying that Gieshala was his first wife, and I can't imagine what happened. It is no wonder that she never liked me. There is no need for me to worry about anything to do with Rollo or the Danes. If I had to bet, I will never see any of them again unless it is in a history book or on the internet. Then I remember that this is not 2022, and there is no internet or Google here. Although I am glad to be back on American soil, I need to figure out how to get back to Audrey and 2022. There seem to be only women here. I don't know how I feel about that.

I wish I had something to give this Indian woman who has been so gracious to share her home and food with me, but I have nothing except a small amount of medical knowledge and my shield maiden clothing that someone else has already taken. I decide to survive here, I will be kind and eager to work. I think about my DNA results and the 25% Native American on my pie chart. It is no surprise that I wound up here. Since I read my Ancestory pie chart, I've landed in England, with the Danes in Finland, and now with the Native Americans. I seem to be following the chart. That leaves the French and Irish unless you counted those on the *Titanic*. What I really want is to be back home with Audrey. I want to be alive in 2022 in America with my only child. I realize that I will always wonder about having a life as a Viking with Rollo Lodbrok and about being his wife, but I feel just as safe here with the Powhatan Indians as I did with him, which isn't saying much. I think of Floke, Geishala, Aud, Ubba, and Naddod. I wasn't really in love with Rollo. I was more fascinated by him and his way of life.

The Powhatan woman motions for me to follow her outside. Once outside, I understand why she has exchanged my shield maiden clothing for this moose hide jacket. It is freezing cold outside. I am totally amazed at how warm the wigwam is.

She shows me a stack of dead cattails that we are to weave into mats for the floor of the wigwam. She shows me how to weave these mats. I learn quickly. Soon, I am making them by myself. They may not look as good as hers do, but they will serve the purpose.

She smiles. I think her smile is better than her snort. She and I may become friends. She seems friendlier than Geishala was.

Suddenly, there is a big noisy group of male Native Americans who enter the camp from the forest. After speaking to another group of women, they make their way to where we are weaving mats. One of the men looks me over. I feel that I am being judged like a prize sheep is judged in a 4-H competition.

My Indian friend has me stand and turns me around for him to get a better view. He nods. I meet his approval. Apparently, he likes what he sees and whatever she says to him. Soon I understand that he has just paid her to purchase me. He hands her a large beaver that was hanging from his waist. She smiles and pushes me toward him.

I find that I may now be the property of an elderly, Indian man, a hunter. I hope that he is kind. I must believe that he is, or I will be in a world of trouble. I hope he isn't looking for a wife. I would rather be his slave. I think of John my husband. I think of Rollo.

The Indian man motions for me to follow him toward the entrance. I look toward the woman who has sold me. She motions for me to stay with her, so I do. They argue. I think it is about the price he has paid for me. She hands him his beaver back. I think of the phrase "Indian giver," but I'm glad because I would rather stay with these women. We walk away from her wigwam toward the sweat wigwam. She drags me inside again. I was just in here yesterday, but I have no way getting out of it. Soon I realize that the Powhatans use the sweat wigwam a few times per week kind of like bathing. I think about all the diseases that the white men brought to the Native Americans and hope these people don't get any from me, but I realize that I have immunity that they don't. I have had vaccines and survived viruses that they haven't had yet.

She removes both my moose hide jacket and hers too. I don't think I should be in this sauna again so soon, but I sit kindly and listen to her story of becoming chief or werowansqua. I understand her hand gestures, but that is all. I smile and remember that the chiefs are female and the lineage is passed down through the female line.

She admires my attentiveness. I've found the key to her heart. I hope. She smiles at me. That is a good sign. She no longer grunts at me. Smiles are universal language.

Soon we exit the sweat lodge and go outside to roll in the snow. She hands me my moose jacket, and I feel its warmth. We move on back toward her wigwam. I wonder if there are other women who live with her. I hope they will be cordial also, but I remember how the English women on the *Titanic* were. I am never well-liked by other women. I have accepted it as a fact of life. Perhaps these Native American women are an exception.

Whenever we enter her wigwam, she shows me my pallet. It is made from a cattail mat and there is my moose hide for cover. Once again, I am exhausted from the sweat lodge.

The sweat lodge has the same effect on me as a sleeping pill. My new friend immediately lays on her pallet and falls asleep. I guess it is her sleeping pill too. I am very sleepy, but I don't feel very secure here. It is hard for me to relax because I have no idea what tonight or tomorrow will being, and I am hungry again. There is no refrigerator to go raid. Eventually with my stomach growling, I fall asleep too. I dream that I'm somewhere in a hospital in a coma. In my dream, I'm hooked to lots of tubes.

Chapter 13

In the early dawn hours, I realize that I am not alone under the moose hide on my pallet. The Native American man who tried to buy me for a beaver is under the moose hide with me, but he is fully dressed in the same hunting clothes that he wore yesterday. He is talking to me in a hushed tone, but I don't understand what he is saying. Finally, I realize that he is trying to wake me without waking the others. I feel like a man is not supposed to be in this wigwam and certainly not in my pallet. I wonder if I should be as afraid as I am, but I realize that if I scream, I will wake all the others who are sleeping in this wigwam, and he hasn't done anything except try to wake me. He has my shield maiden pants and boots in his hand. I want them. He wants me to dress in these under my moose hide jacket. He is trying to explain to me that we will be traveling north where it is very cold. I ask him if we will be going to Massachusetts. The Massachusetts are another tribe, and in 2022, it is the name of a state. Then I realize that there aren't any states yet, so he can't know where I mean. Somehow I figure that we are going up there. I don't know why I feel that way, but I feel that if I make it that far alive, I will be sold to someone from Salem. I've been called a witch so many times, so being sold in Salem seems appropriate. I don't figure that he means to keep me for very long. I remember what I've learned from studying the history of the Salem Witch Trials and what caused them to think those folks were witches. I think about the first little girls having eaten barley, rye, and wheat bread with fungus on it that caused them to act strangely as if possessed. I wonder if the bread or cereal didn't have a pungent smell. I will be certain not to eat their bread, but never eating bread is like being on a no carb diet making a piece of white bread taste as good as a piece of cake.

Thinking of bread makes me realize how hungry that I am. The fish and nuts that woman had given me yesterday are long gone. Suddenly, I realize that these Native American people eat only when they are hungry and not the American three meals per day. That is why none of the folks are overweight. It is intermittent fasting, the new trend in weight loss. My stomach growls loudly. It is embarrassing. I will take me some time to not being hungry on cue for the three American meals per day. The Native American man has heard my stomach growl and smiles at me. He reaches into a pouch that he has bound to his waist and hands me some roasted fish and nuts.

I eat them hungrily. He smiles again. Just as we are about to leave, the chief wakes and blocks the doorway challenging him. He hands her a large basket of things he has brought to pay her for me. The one beaver hadn't been enough. The basket contains three deerskins, a large basket of sea shells like the ones on my moose skin coat, some copper, and a large basket of shelled corn. It also contains my shield maiden clothes. I am amazed and surprised at the amount he is willing to pay for me, and I can't figure out why I'm so valuable to them. She looks at all the loot, and I think that she is going to make the trade. Suddenly, she shakes her head and turns him down. I am surprised. From his body language I can tell that he is very angry. He gathers up his loot and puts it back into the large basket. He throws back the skin over the doorway where it hangs flapping open, letting the cold inside. She throws up her hands in disgust and points outside for him to leave. She utters some words angrily. He heaves the basket to his shoulder and exits, leaving my shield maiden clothes. The woman chief grabs the skin covering the door and pulls it closed. She is daring him to come back.

By now the entire wigwam of people is awake from the noise and cold air and all them are looking at me. I realize that they would have taken his loot and sent me out the door with him. I don't understand why the chief didn't. They don't either.

It is still dark outside, so we snuggle back into our pallets. I am still hungry now, and I'm too confused to go back to sleep for a long time. Finally, I drift off and wake to find that small little girl has once again snuggled under the moose hide with me. I realize that there are only females in this wigwam. I like that. I realize that same man had angered the chief by sneaking inside her wigwam and trying to buy or steal me even with an exorbitant price.

Maybe her anger came from his actions and is not about me, or she needs another slave. Me. As far as I can tell, none of these women are her slaves. Right before I fall asleep again, my toes tingle again. The pain feels as strong as it had in the beginning, and I feel like needles are being stuck into my arms. I know there will be bruises on my arms tomorrow. My breathe comes in short, raspy gasps. My head aches. The gasps wake the little Indian girl who shares my bed. I wonder which of the women is her mother. I wonder what is wrong with me and causing the bruises and shortness of breath. I wondered why I am here and how to leave and get back to 2022 and Audrey. I hug the small child closer to me. She snuggles and goes back to sleep.

The morning comes quickly and as I had predicted, I have large bruises on my arms near the inside of my elbow. There is also a large bruise on the top of one of my hands. I notice the chief looking at my bruised arms. I hope she won't throw me back into the sweat lodge again today because of them. Perhaps she will think the Indian man who had tried to steal me had bruised me. My pale skin bruises more easily than her dark skin, or the bruises show more.

When we go outdoors, the sky is clear and no snow is falling. I raise my face to the sun feeling its warmth. I remember being on the *Titanic* and feeling the sun on my face whenever I sneaked above deck and sat with Molly Brown. I had figured it would be the last time that I would feel the sunshine. It wasn't. She gathers more cattails, and we go back inside to weave them into mats.

We weave cattail mats most all day until my fingers bleed. I never complain. The other women in the wigwam watch me closely as if waiting for me to complain, but none are cruel or even rude to me. I figured that now I belong to the werowansqua or chief, and they are not bold enough to be rude to me whenever she is around. They seemed to be amazed that I don't complain. It is like they respect me more.

I realize how much of communication isn't really verbal. Body language and other looks are more than half of the communication between humans, and these Native American women didn't really trust or like me in the beginning. I'm not certain that I would have trusted any of them had the tables been turned. I don't think they understand why the chief had kept me either. I am sure that it wasn't to weave cattail mats.

Finally, the next morning, I get a clue. She waits until the other women and children leave the wigwam and hands me my shield maiden clothes. She instructs me to dress in them. They are dry. Then with hand signals, she tells me to show her how to defend myself. She wants me to teach her how to defend myself like Rollo the Viking had taught me. She wants to be a shield maiden. The only problem is that I had no shield or sword. They had been lost in the sea. Then I have a brilliant idea. I show her with my hand signals that we need the shields and swords.

Suddenly, she must have the same idea that I do. There were shields and swords left on the beach where Rollo, and I washed ashore when I had been taken by the two Native American men. Perhaps the weapons are still there.

We dress in our moose skin coats over our other leather clothes and make our way across the forest to the coastal plain where we'd washed ashore. The weapons are gone. The beach is clean. Someone else had removed all the debris from the Vikings and Rollo's ship back to it's natural clean state. Perhaps the tide had washed the beach clean, but I didn't think the swords would have floated back out to sea, so someone else had taken them.

But I have an idea. These Powhatans had knives, but having an iron sword made by the Danes would have been considered a treasure of great value like the sword of King Arthur. What they didn't have was the expertise or materials to make swords. They were still using stone tomahawks instead of iron. I don't know what to do, but I do realize that my value to her has gone down. So in the sand, I draw a shield. At least we can make a wooden shield of some kind and strap the wood together with leather cords. We could fight with the longest knives and extend them by strapping them to carved wooden bases, a kind of makeshift sword. Apparently the chief knows that a war with someone is imminent. Now, I am to become a teacher of shield maidens. I've never fought against anyone except Rollo. I pointed to my shield maiden clothes and then to her to show her that tight fitting clothing would be necessary instead of the tunics and moose coats she wears. We had to make shields, swords, and shield maiden leather pants, boots, and shirts. She should have kept the deer hides that man wanted to trade for me. My knowledge makes me more valuable. I feel good about that.

I have nothing to make a pattern or draw on except the sand. I have no paper and no pens or pencils, so I draw in the smooth wet sand and explain each step to the chief until I think she understands. This woman, the chief of the Powhatans, is now my friend. At least, we can copy my shield maiden clothing using the actual clothes as patterns. The women will need shield maiden boots too. The winter time is perfect for teaching them to fight because in the summer, they plant fields of corn, beans, and squash. These foods are their summer menu, and we have no way to preserve much of it except the corn. We dry the corn. Planting is good exercise, but they don't have the time to do both train and plant.

After drawing in the sand for over an hour, we are ready to go back to her wigwam. My internal clock has gotten as good as the chief's. At least, I can keep up with the hours if not the days. I have forgotten how long I have been here. I know it has been many days. Some of them have been enjoyable, especially with Tiny Bird. I still miss Audrey and 2022. The clouds have moved in and hidden the sun, leaving a shining rim around the edges of the clouds. I notice things of nature more than I did before I came to live with the Native Americans. I don't miss the television, computer, or internet. Suddenly, a heavy snow begins to fall. I have never seen snow on the beach before. It accumulates quickly wiping out my drawings but it doesn't wipe out the ideas in our minds. The chief wants to be able to protect ourselves and the tribe. I desperately want to return to my daughter and my old life.

On our way back through the forest to the wigwam, I realize that my knowledge of the history of the Powhatan war is lacking. I can't remember if it is within the tribe or a war with another tribe that she fears, but she knows. The chief knows who we are waiting to fight. I don't think who the war is with matters. A war is a war. The fact that she wants my knowledge the Danes taught me about fighting makes me have more status. The woman chief wants to keep me in her wigwam. Right now, I am grateful.

By the time we enter her village and wigwam, it is already getting late. My stomach rumbles loud enough for everyone in the wigwam to hear. The small Indian girl giggles when she hears it. She calls me, "Growl One." I laugh with her. They call her Tiny Bird.

We eat fish and nuts and then settle into our pallets. The food tastes good, and the little girl and I snuggle in to sleep. I think of Aud, the Danish baby whose mother thought she was a changeling. I hope she is surviving. Soon Tiny Bird is snoring lightly next to me. Since there were no windows in the wigwam, it is difficult to know what time of day it is, but I think we have gone to bed early.

The chief, however, has an internal clock. She wakes us a little before daylight. We have lots to do today including gathering material for shields, swords, and shield maiden clothing. All of it can't be accomplished in one day. It will take weeks to make shields and swords for everyone. Perhaps other women will make the shield maiden clothes. I do not know how to sew, especially leather.

Chapter 14

Three Indian women, the chief, and I truck into the forest carrying only tomahawk axes and sticks with burning fire on the end. They look like flambeau. I think we are going to build a fire to stay warm. I find that limbs aren't hacked off the trees with the tomahawks like I thought they would be, they are burned off with fire. The process is ingenious really. We let the fire do the hard labor. After the chief gets several limbs burned off and we have a pile, we determine the length we need for the shields and soon have a large pile to carry back to the camp. One of the women selects long poles small enough for them to be fashioned into sword handles, but strong enough to use. By noon, we haul the poles back to the front of the chief's wigwam. Then I see that women have collected deer skins for the shield maiden clothes. The only difference in these skins and my shield maiden clothes is that there is deer hair left on one side of the deer skins. We put the hair side to the inside. Tanning hides is time consuming, so we use what we have. Thankfully, the women didn't deconstruct my shield maiden clothing for a pattern while we are gathering the wood for the shields. I am so happy that it is still intact. I love my shield maiden clothing because Rollo gave it to me.

The chief has designated women to sew shield maiden clothes and others to help bind the shields together with leather bands. I am to make the first shield as a prototype. We take willow poles of the same length and tie them to cross pieces with deer hide strips. I know these aren't as strong as the Danes' shields and may not protect us from tomahawk blows, but they may protect us from arrows. Once they understand the concept for making shields, I move on to showing some others how to strap their knives to longer handles for swords.

By nightfall, I am as tired as I've ever been. We have six extra shield maiden outfits besides mine and seven shields and makeshift swords. We eat a meal of roasted deer meat, nuts, and corn patties. Tiny Bird and I snuggle together under my moose hide, and I fall asleep quickly. I am exhausted from our long day of work. I dream of being married to Rollo Lodbrok.

The chief wakes me at sunrise, and I sneak outside to find that a light snow mixed with sleet is falling. I long for a warm cozy fire and a cup of hot chocolate or a cup of coffee from Starbucks. It has been so long. Then I remember where I am. I really don't want to train women in the snow, but it may be snowing when the war begins. I have no way of knowing. Wars don't wait for beautiful weather. I don't even know who or why we will be fighting. I have a feeling that I will fight in another war before I get home or back to 2022. The chief doesn't explain and my history lessons didn't extend that far to details of the Powhatans. Shield maidens need super upper body strength, so we begin by lifting large rocks. These Powhatan women act as if I've lost my mind. Maybe I have. Lifting weights is a 2022 American exercise for modern women, but it works. These shields we have fashioned are not as heavy as my Danish shield was, and they won't hold up to much. I wish Rollo was here to help me. He would whip these ladies into shape fast, and I'm certain that they would rather be trained by a good-looking man than by me. These Native Americans will be fighting settlers and most likely men who won't be expecting shields. I hope it isn't the Vikings that the chief expects to return. They will be expecting bows and arrows and tomahawks. I have slits and tabs fashioned in the shield maiden tunics for securing the tomahawks and our makeshift swords. I think of Velcro. Velcro tabs would make it possible to secure lots of weapons. The more weapons that are available; the better. So if our tomahawk is dropped, we would still have our knife or our makeshift sword.

In the forest, I notice some poisonous mushrooms growing on a rotten log near a ditch. They are called *Galerina marginata*, but I see no point in trying to teach these women the modern American name of the mushrooms. We can cover the tips of our swords and tomahawks with the poison. Our enemies will die if we can injure them. Maybe now; maybe later, but with this poison, they will die. I am never certain exactly who our enemies are supposed to be. I don't know if they were within the Powhatan tribe, those from another tribe, or even men from another part of the world like Rollo or Leif Erickson.

I train with the Native American Powhatan women for six weeks, but a war never comes in that length of time. The spring temperatures bring men to prepare the fields for us to plant. They remove the large weeds and saplings. I long for tractors and tillers. Planting is hard work, so we stop training as shield maidens and become farmers. We plant corn, beans, and squash. Everyone helps even the little children who act like scarecrows even before the plants come up. They shoo away the crows and other birds that try to dig up the seeds. I am not exactly sure how they plan to keep the deer and raccoons out of the fields at night, but I'm certain they have a method. I think about the organic movement in America. The Powhatans are truly organic farmers. Their foods are wholesome and without dyes and added chemicals from start to finish. There are absolutely zero obese people in the tribes.

I have been gone from my America 2021 for so long that I would almost kill for an order of fries and a McDonald's Big Mac, organic or not. These Native Americans roast their meat. They have no way to grind it to make burgers and no oil for frying French fries. Come to think of it, they have no potatoes that I have seen.

During our down time while waiting for the crops to grow, we paint figures on our bodies; and during the warm, damp weather, we cover ourselves with bear fat to repel the mosquitoes. I don't know why the bear fat smells antiseptic to me, but it does. Some of the men have animal tatoos. The women have floral designs. I wonder what they use for ink. I wonder how healthy this body paint is. There is no agency to check the safety of things like the FDA. Although we sometimes wear our shield maiden suits, the warm weather makes them too hot and the hair we left on the inside of the leather makes you sweat. On the hot days, we trade our leather suits for grass garments that reminded me of Hawaii, although I have never been.

Finally, one warm day whenever I go walking alone on the beach near the ocean, I see the tips of sails on the horizon. My heart skips a beat. I wonder if Rollo has come back for me. He is my husband, but I am dead. He thinks. Then I see the entire ship. The flag they fly is English. I knew that they were set to appear, but I didn't know exactly when. There is no calendar here and certainly no CNN or other news or talking head news predictors. I wonder if these are the people we fight in war. Of course, I'm disappointed that it isn't Rollo in a Viking ship. We never even had a honeymoon. I hope there won't be a war. I think that these Englishmen will have muskets. We do not. The Native Americans' only advantage is that they know the lay of the land. They know how to survive here. The English do not.

The tide brings the ship closer to the shore. I move toward the forest to hide in a clump of trees across the beach. It looks as if they have dropped an anchor because their ship stops moving.

I turn to run back to the Indian camp to tell my friend the chief about the English ship, but I am captured by two strong arms over my chest and then my arms are tied and my mouth covered. The same Native American man who tried to buy me months ago had grabbed me and twisted my arms behind my back. Because of the Englishmen, I do not cry out. He may not kill me. They will. My grass clothing rustles in the breeze. We had spent the summer farming, and he hadn't been around. I thought he had moved to some other area of the country or died. I was wrong. Other men had helped clear the grass and weeds from the fields and patches, but not him. He drags me toward the north. This time he has no basket of goodies to pay the chief for me. This time he has stolen me. All at once the view of the smaller boat coming on shore disappears from my sight. The women in our camp are going to get a surprise.

I think of Tiny Bird. I try to think where she is this morning. It is Tiny Bird's morning to be the scarecrow in the cornfield. A cornfield that is about three feet tall. Her tiny statue might not be seen over the tops of the corn. Maybe she will hide. Maybe the men won't ever know she is there, but if the women are killed, she will be left alone. I worry about her like I worried about Aud with the Vikings.

Then I slowly lose consciousness. I feel myself being dragged along toward the north. My brain becomes foggy. I can't think. All the things that have happened to me flash through my memory, Audrey and the Mother's Day ancestry DNA present, the flight to England and the car accident, sailing on the *Titanic* and sinking, being rescued by the Vikings and marrying Rollo, being shipwrecked in America and the Powhatan's, and now being kidnapped and dragged toward the north up the beach. The man dragging me across the sand and into the edge of the forest must have drugged me with something. I can't wake myself. My thinking is foggy. I think of people in 2020 talking about a Covid 19 brain fog. I am in a brain fog, but it isn't Covid or 2020. The sky fades away again. I remember being hungry. It is time for me to be transported to another location. I dream of looking at my DNA pie chart. I remember the Native American slice of my pie chart. I remember one of my teacher friends calling it a circle graph. My stomach rumbles loudly. I hope someone from the Powhatan tribe is near enough to hear it. Of course, it they are that near, they would probably be helping him kidnap me. He doesn't need any help. I kick at the man dragging me. One foot, the one with the toes that tingle most of the time, strikes his naked shin. I scream in pain as he screams too. He hits me with something. The blood trickles down my face. I taste the saltiness of it. But still he drags me toward the north, he most likely will sell me to another Indian tribe. Since I don't know what year it is, and my remembrance of history is sketchy at this point, I figure that the English had arrived in the early 1600's. I need and want to be back in 2022 with Audrey. That and staying alive is my goal. In 2022, kidnapping is a crime. There are people to help me in 2022 and laws.

I wonder what my price will be this time, but I really don't care. I feel something being shoved in my mouth. My lips are dry. They stick to whatever he is shoving into my mouth. He has gagged me. It feels as if a stick has been shoved down my throat and into my stomach. I gag again. I lose consciousness.

Then suddenly I wake and walk to the microphone, I am singing happy birthday to President John F. Kennedy. I have made them wait for a while before my dress was sewed on. I wear no underwear under it. You can see through it, and it is so tight that none of my curves are a mystery. Dressing this way is part of my persona of changing myself from Norma Jeane Baker to Marilyn Monroe. It got the President's attention, his brother's too. I've even captured Frank Sinatra's attention. Tonight I'm singing Happy Birthday for the President. It is a treat that I won't ever forget.

Later, I'm going to a birthday party for him. I will be slipped inside so no one recognizes me. I've taken too many pills for my nerves. I need to sleep. I find a couch in a quiet corner to take a quick nap. I kick off my shoes and massage my tingling toes. These pointed shoes are killing my feet. Sleep comes quickly.

Then suddenly I wake and find that I'm on trial for witchcraft. I am no longer is 1961. There are English men and women around me. Mostly, in the courtroom, there are English men around me, but a few women are on trial with me. The men wear knee length black pants, tall socks or leggings, and shoes with large metal buckles. Their dress reminds me of costumes my classmates wore in the Thanksgiving play when I was in junior high school. Around their shoulders, they wear dark colored capes. Some of their shirts have large white ruffles at the neck and at the wrist. Some wear big white collars like the Puritans. I remember their pictures from a history book. Some wear waistcoats; some wear shaped-tall crowns, with flat-brimmed hats. I feel like I'm in a movie about the Puritans. I stand before them. I am on trial. Just as I predicted while I lived with the Powhatan's, I am on trial for being a witch. At least my history is clear at this point. The date is February 1692. It is as if the digits were transposed. I do not know how to return to 2022, but I won't mention being from 2022 to these strange Puritan men and women.

I'm so concerned with these men's costumes that I forget about my own, but I'm not wearing the grass clothing that I was wearing whenever I saw the English ship off the coast of Virginia and was kidnapped by that Native American man, and I'm not wearing the see thru dress that Marilyn Monroe wore while singing to President John Kennedy. Well, in 2022, that beach where the English were landing is called Virginia, but now, I'm in Salem, Massachusetts, and I'm one of the people on trial for witchcraft. There are about two hundred of us. Most are women, but a few are men. The grass clothing would be offensive to the Puritans, and so would have Marilyn's dress. I long for my shield maiden clothing. I long for Rollo to get me out of here. I long for my shield and my sword that Rollo bought me. Before I got here, I vowed never to eat the bread here, but it seems that I was sold to these people after being kidnapped by that Native American man. Of course, I don't remember if I was given any bread or not.

"This court will come to order." The judge says, rapping on this desk with a wooden gavel. That tradition is still used in 2022. I watch his large white collar flop up to his chin. I could strangle him with that collar. He looks like he is wimpy, a kind of Barney Fife looking character. "This court will come to order," he screams. I think he may have eaten some of that moldy bread, too.

I am one of the ones on trial next, but I get to witness the trial of the accused woman before me. Maybe I will learn what not to say from her answers. We sit quietly in order of who will testify or be questioned next. I try to remember what actually did happen. I arrived here and was welcomed into the home of John Indian and Tituba. He is South American, and she's from Barbados. Somehow Barbados reminds me of an island on a soap opera like Days of Our Lives that is controlled by the Dimeras. I don't know why.

The Puritians think we confer with the Devil. I think if we did, we would band together and overcome this wimpy court of wimpy men. In this group of people accused of witchcraft, there are only two men. I wonder how they would react if I arrived here dressed as Marilyn Monroe of 1961. I would probably be flogged. I'm certain I would be branded a witch immediately.

The woman before me testifying for herself is asked to show a mole that's on her arm. Apparently, the mole has grown into the shape of an animal. I think they say it looks like a dog. I want to scream that she needs to see a dermatologist. I think of Marilyn's painted on mole. This lady has carcinoma, but dermatologists aren't part of the medical community in 1692. I'm thinking the medical community here is no smarter than the medical community of the

Powhatans or of The Vikings. Finally, this woman on trial screams like a banshee. I think her nerves got the best of her. She is removed from the courtroom. I hear whispers that she will be taken to the nearby river or sea and cast into the water. If she tries to swim, she will be ruled a witch and hung. Otherwise, she will drown. That hardly seems fair, but the Puritans are now known for fairness. There is no way for her to win. How can drowning let you know if she is a witch? It is enough to make you scream like a banshee. I hope that isn't my fate. Although almost drowning usually gets me transported to another time and place. Maybe I'll go back to 1961 or even better 2022.

Once she has been dragged out of the courtroom, I am led to the witness stand. I don't resist. I don't care to be shot or clubbed by these wimpy looking men. I am aware that my American accent will be detected unfavorably. These people are English. I think about my DNA pie chart. This is not exactly how I wanted to visit the English. I wonder which part related to Marilyn Monroe. Probably the connection was President Kennedy and the Irish Catholics.

"State your name," the inquiring Puritan judge asks.

"Heidi Lodbrok." The courtroom becomes quiet. They have detected my accent.

"Are you a friend of the Devil?"

"Of course, not," I reply. "Are you?"

"Did you ask the Devil to help you with magical spells and potions?"

"No. If I did, you would not be asking me these stupid questions, and I would have married President John F. Kennedy, or at least his brother Bobby.

"We have been given testimony that you can turn yourself into an owl. Can you turn yourself into an owl? Does the Devil help you turn into an owl? Who is this President Kennedy?"

"No. Who told you that? Have you been reading Harry Potter? Owls deliver the mail." I knew that whatever my answers were, he didn't care. He had made up his mind already. My sassy answers couldn't help or hurt me now. He had no idea who or what I was talking about. I did get his attention by mentioning President Kennedy although he had no idea who he was. Rumors abound among those accused that he was a friend of the political party in charge and not a friend of the current Reverend of the church whose slave is also on trial for witchcraft. Her name is Tituba. According to her, there was a family feud brewing in this town of Salem, and it wasn't the funny game show with Steve Harvey that I used to watch on television in 2022. This feud was real and deadly. The Reverend and his enslaved cook had taken me in. Mostly, she was my friend. He allowed me to live in his house as a show of his charity. It looked good to the community and his congregation. It was political. Why is everything political? However I had arrived here, I was included in the feud now. I knew the outcome of this trial from reading history, but of course, being able to tell the future was the sign of a witch.

I also had been making potions and salves for the people I now lived with from my medical knowledge. I didn't know whom to trust, but I already knew that I was going to be tried as a witch. I had a premonition even while I was in England and on the *Titanic*. I had heard rumblings in the town of Salem. I was different. I was educated. I knew that the trials would happen. I predicted them.

Anyway there was no way that I could live with Tituba and get passed over as a witch. She made amulets to ward off evil spirits, but all wearing the amulet did for me was get me branded a witch with her. I had even worn my amulet that she made for me inside my blouse, but it gave off a pungent smell alerting passersby. Of course, those little girls who either have epilepsy or who had eaten fungus on their bread are included in this trial.

Tituba and I had spent several afternoons with these children. She taught them spells and love potions. It was all in fun. One of the girls had a boyfriend that she wanted to impress with a love potion.

"If I were an owl, I would fly out of here." I state simply and flap my arms like wings.

"You were seen late one night wandering into Salem. You seemed to be disoriented or in a trance. Can you tell me where you had been?"

"Well, let's see. I may have been living with the Powhatans or at a party with President and Bobby Kennedy, or I may have been on the *Titanic* or on a ship with The Vikings."

The judge looked perplexed. He didn't understand half of what I was saying.

"No. I cannot," I answer. I knew that the state of my life at this particular time was unbelievable even to me.

"Since you are unable to tell us from where you came, you are now convicted as a witch. You will be hanged by the neck until dead."

"Oh, not burned at the stake? Actually, I did tell you. You didn't understand anything I said. In American movies, witches from Salem are burned at the stake." Why can't I keep my smart mouth closed? Must I taunt these men?

Suddenly a loud roar fills the courtroom. No one here except me knows what a movie is.

"Silence," the judge screams hysterically and beats the wooden gavel on his desk. "This woman has definitely been consulting with the Devil."

"And President Kennedy," I say. "But you are the hysterical one."

I am dragged from the witness stand across the rough wooden floor. The only smooth areas of the floor are those used most often. I'm thinking how hard these rough boards would be to clean and how rough they would be on bare feet with splinters. I'm certain that bare feet are against the Puritan dress code. That would be too much skin showing. I am thrown into a small room with no windows, but I can still hear the activity and what is said in the courtroom. I wonder if I can hear them, can they hear me? Next on the witness stand is Tituba, the slave of the local minister. She says she is from Barbados. I had been living here in Salem with her and her husband John at his house. Tituba is originally from somewhere in South America and as a teen was sold to someone in Barbados where the Reverend acquired her. I have explained all that happened to me to Tituba, but I feel that it was a mistake. She says it is all a dream. She says that I'm not really here. She practices voodoo that she learned in Barbados and knows how to place spells on people. Some in the town want to get rid of her owner as minister, but he has purchased his own home and doesn't live in their parsonage. They can't evict him, so they are going after his slave. I feel it is racially motivated and political. If this was America 2022 or even 1961, it definitely would be. All who have been accused of being witches are poor and uneducated except me. I am different. Because they don't know me and because I am friends with Tituba, I was arrested as a witch. Tituba knows that I'm from 2022, but they do not. I hope she doesn't tell them.

I listen closely. They ask her stupid questions such as the following: Does she dance with the Devil when he visits the minister's house? Did she feed a witch cake made with urine to some little girls? Where were she and I going the moonlight night we were picked up? Why is she always roaming around on the nights with a full moon? Did she teach some little girls to ride on brooms? Did she teach me to ride a broom? Does she know President Kennedy?

Finally, she is so angry that she begins to tell them what they want to know. She tells them about the Devil. She tells them about red and black rats, red sand black dogs, and me. She tightens the noose around her neck and mine. She tells them that I'm a world traveler from 2022. The Queen of the World Travelers is what she calls me. A huge frantic roar goes around the room, so they really think I'm a witch too. They think the Devil has come to inhabit Salem. Soon, she too is convicted of being a witch.

She is thrown into the small room with me, and at least, we were not thrown into the river to sink or swim, yet. I remembered seeing pictures of women being strapped to a wooden seat and dipped under the water and left to see if they drowned. I am thinking that with Tituba's help she and I may escape, but I haven't figured how yet.

Suddenly, the door is thrown open again and two girls, some relation to the Reverend, are thrown into the room with us. These are the same two who told the authorities and the Reverend that Tituba was teaching them witchcraft. I'm certain that being held with them inside this small room isn't going to turn out well. I wanted to talk with Tituba about escaping, but how could I with these two snitches in here too. The room is really too small to whisper without being heard.

Tituba and I move over to a corner of the room away from the snitches. My history lesson on the Salem witch trials is lacking on a few points such as who was hanged and who was set free. My stomach begins to rumble. I am hungry. I remember that I have a pouch of dried fish and nuts around my waist. The men who arrested us hadn't searched us very well. I learned to carry food with me from the Powhatans. I open the pouch and share with Tituba. While eating, I remember that there are matches in my amulet bag instead of potions or poison like Tituba carries in hers. Apparently, the Powhatans are more prepared than Marilyn Monroe was.

There are bags filled with hay strewn around the room for us to use as beds or to sit on. They remind me of beds for dogs. This pen looks more for an animal than a human. Bags of hay are the only comfortable item added. I notice that there aren't even any pails for use as a bathroom. These pallets would go up in a big flame, but since we have no windows or other way for the smoke to escape, we would all probably die. The entire building would burn and possibly the town. Burning the town of Salem wasn't in the history books, and if I've learned anything, you can't change history. This is a room within the courthouse building for the courtroom. The courtroom is inside a large wooden building next to other wooden buildings, houses, and stores. The opening to the outside is in the courtroom.

Finally, the two snitches cry themselves to sleep. I feel bad for not having shared my food with them. They are probably hungry too. According to history these two had eaten rye or some other bread with fungus to make them have fits, or they are epileptic. No one is certain exactly what happened.

Proof of witches was never established. The only thing that is certain in the history books is that only poor or enslaved people were accused. My gut feeling is that all of us will be freed, but I don't know how soon. Because of this feeling in my gut, I am not as frightened as I need to be. I need to get out of here and back to Audrey in 2022, but definitely I do not know how. Like the Native Americans, perhaps after three or four days without food, I will have a vision that tells me how to return home.

Tituba assures me that all my traveling is only a dream. She says that I will wake. I want to talk to her more about it. With the two snitches in here with us, how can we discuss my returning to 2022. My accent is American and Tituba's is Indian or from Barbados, so we don't communicate well. Somehow, I know that Tituba knows how I can return. I really want to know how. I feel that my ancestry DNA adventure isn't finished yet. I feel that I have more places to travel and more dangerous situations to endure, so dying here while accused of being a witch isn't happening. I hope.

Finally, I slip off to sleep and dream about needles being stuck in my arms and adhesive being ripped off my skin. My toes tingle, and I dream of having a high temperature. My breathing is labored, and my gut rumbles. I feel like throwing up. I wonder if it is possible to dream while dreaming or if I'm in a dream as Tituba said I was.

I wake to find that the room is filled with smoke. One of the snitches or Tituba has set fire to her sack of hay pallet.

I rush to the door and pound loudly. Finally, a man wearing the traditional Puritan costume unlocks the door. I don't know that I expected him to still be so dressed up, but getting fully dressed is a religious requirement. Coming to our rescue in his underwear as a Puritan is unacceptable, whether we die or not. Stinky smoke fills the courtroom. He rushes to beat the flaming pallet out with a broom. Another man opens the door of the courtroom to the outside to let the stinky smoke escape. More people who are considered witches are on trial tomorrow. While all this is happening, I quickly slip through the door to the outside and into the street. The smoke is thick, and they don't notice me or that I'm gone. With all the commotion in the pen where we are housed, my exit is not noticed. I slip through an alley across the street from the courthouse instead of one beside the courthouse. The courthouse is built from wood like a saltbox house with straight sides and two floors. I guess the Puritans sleep on the second floor. The streets are deserted as I slip away and into the forest. I have nowhere to go and no one to help me. I am alone.

Chapter 15

Quickly, I make my way back to the Minister's house. I need warm clothing. Since Tituba and I had so many nighttime excursions, I know how to slip into the Minister's house without waking anyone except the dog, and the dog likes me. I go to my sleeping area to get some warm clothing. I find woolen skirts and capes. I take a pair of boots. I long for my leather shield maiden clothing, but it is long gone. The commotion in the town has reached here, so I exit the house quickly out the back way and slip into the thickness of the forest. A light rain has started to fall. It will help prevent the spread of the courthouse fire. I am glad. I never wanted anyone to get hurt.

I do not know where I am going. I do not know anyone who might help me except Tituba's husband John Indian. They lived in a cabin deep in the woods part of the time. She and I had gone there many times on our nighttime excursions, so I make my way to their cabin.

So far, no one is following me. When I reach John's cabin, I knock lightly on the door. I think it is around two o'clock in the morning. I don't pound on the door because then John might think I am from the town of Salem to arrest him. While I am standing quietly at the front door waiting for him to open it, John slips out the back door. He shows up behind me. "Hello," he says in his hard to understand South American accent. "How can I help you, Heidi?"

I turn toward the sound of his voice.

"I escaped. Tituba didn't, but she is okay. Will you help me?"

"I'm getting Charles Montague to pay her bail tomorrow. She will be free then. Then we are going back to South America or as far away from here as possible. Tituba is not a witch. Not in the way they think. She does know some remedies and ways to use herbs. This is a political struggle between two rich influential families. It has nothing to do with us anyway. Mr. Montague says the governor is going to put a stop to it. He needs to hurry."

"John, I need to disappear."

"I will help you. Let me get my things. I will take you downriver in the canoe. Then I must come back to rescue Tituba."

"John, I don't want you to think I'm a witch, but I know that Tituba gets away. I mean that you will be able to get her out of jail."

"I remember that she said you were from the future. Tell me how you got out of the locked room, and she didn't if you aren't a witch." We walk to the river and load the canoe that is sitting on the bank where he left it.

"Someone started a fire in our pallets. I beat on the door until one of the Puritans opened it. While they were beating out the fire with a broom, I sneaked out the door to the outside that had been opened to let the smoke escape. They were intent on keeping the building from burning. Those two young girls who started this whole mess had been locked in that room with us. Tituba was trying to save them. I slipped out and ran to the Minister's house to get some warm clothes. Then I ran here. I don't think anyone followed."

Off in the distance down the trail, we hear dogs barking. "Don't be so sure," John says. "They are using the dogs to trail you. We must leave in haste."

I get into the front of the canoe and he gets in the back. He shoves off from the bank. As he paddles downriver, I hear the men and the dogs approaching his cabin. Then they make their way past his cabin to where we got into the canoe, but we are about a half mile ahead of them, and they don't have a boat.

I see lights moving along the riverbank. I don't think they will be able to catch up to us. I don't think that I'm that important to them. I hope not. I know I don't make it into their history books. We easily make our way downriver with John's paddling and the current. I don't know where he is taking me, but I have a strong feeling that I'm set for another adventure. I hope this one is to 2022.

"Hold on, Heidi," John says. He pronounces my name like Floke did. "We will get out before the rapids." I think about Aud. I think about Tiny Bird and the Powhatans. I think about Rollo, but mostly I want to be back with Audrey.

I hear a loud rushing of water over rocks like rapids, but there are lights near the bank. Someone is camping near the rapids. John Indian doesn't move to the bank. We stay in the river. The roar becomes deafening. I am afraid, not to drown, but to be banged against the rocks. I feel paralyzed to do anything. I feel as if my lungs are filling with water. "Can you swim?" I yell as our canoe is torn apart by the rocks. But I don't get an answer.

I feel the cold water swallowing me. It reminds me of the sinking of the *Titanic*. I feel as if I'm drowning. My head aches. John Indian is not visible. I pray that he didn't drown helping me escape. I remember almost drowning whenever the *Titanic* sunk, then almost drowning when the storm crashed Rollo's Viking ship onto the beach. Now, John Indian's canoe has crashed on the rapids. But I am not dead. Not yet. But it definitely is bad luck, especially for him and Tituba.

I am hauled on shore. Perhaps out of a river. I feel like a few days pass before I know where I am. I guess my internal clock is still ticking. Is this real or am I dreaming like Tituba says?

Off in the distance, I hear gunfire. Then I hear a louder boom like a canon. I hear the whoops of what sounds like savages. I must be with the Native Americans again. I'm not dead, but where am I? I wake. I open my eyes.

I look down at my clothes. I'm wearing the clothing of an Indian maiden. My clothing is made from leather and resembles the shield maiden suit that Rollo purchased for me. I have a short leather tunic over the leather pants. I think this outfit is Sioux. It is decorated with tiny beads. I look around. We are camped near a river, and there are a few tall hills to the east, covered in a tall grass that flows in the wind. I am with Sitting Bull's people, and it is 1876. We are at the Little Bighorn in eastern Montana. I remember what happened here from reading history. I want to tell Sitting Bull the outcome of this battle, but I don't. He and Crazy Horse are preparing to fight Custer. His is another language that I don't speak. I wonder how much English they know. I remember my ancestry DNA results from the Mother's Day present in 2021 that Audrey purchased.

Across on the hill, Lt. Col. George Armstrong Custer is recklessly waiting to carry out his orders --to scout out the encampments of some Sioux and Cheyenne near the Little Bighorn river. He is supposed to wait to attack. He won't. I know. He wants medals and recognition. He will get them. Custer divides his men and sends Captain Frederick Benteen with 120 troops to scout far to the field. Then he commands Major Marcus A. Reno and about 120 men across the Little Bighorn river to attack the Indian encampment from the south. With his 600 troops depleted, he still assigns 129 men to guard the pack train.

There are thousands of Native Americans here. There is Sitting Bull and Crazy Horse. Custer is outnumbered by thousands.

Reno's men attack, dismount, and start to fight Native Americans for their first time ever. The only trees nearby are down in the valley near the river banks. Custer begins moving his men to the east bank of the Native American village. By 4 P.M. his men are stretched out in the open as wave after wave of Native American men under the direction of Crazy Horse fight back. They kill scores of soldiers. The soldiers wave across the plains like the grass blows in the wind. Their spirit is all that remains. Blood covers the hills. With that Custer couldn't retreat. Although the Native Americans thought Custer's men were some of the bravest they had seen, the battle ended about dusk. General Custer and most of his men are dead. All that is left for Custer is for someone to erect the monument he so desperately wants and for others to see the blood and bodies of American soldiers covering the plains near Little Bighorn everywhere.

When the battle is over, I move out with Sitting Bull's band toward Canada as if I am one of them. I try to blend in. It is on the way that they realize that I am American woman. No one asks how I got here. They seem to think I am spiritual like the eagles or the wind. Maybe I am. I am part Native American. I like being with them.

I wonder where I will wake next. Of the Native Americans I've lived with, I liked the Powhatans best. I miss Tiny Bird, but she is in a different time and place. With the Powhatans, I was mostly with females.

While traveling with Sitting Bull, I am summoned to his side to give him advice as a seer. He claims to have had a vision about a Ghost Dance. I am part of it. Not wanting to disappoint him, I do not confirm or deny his vision. He has my admiration as a great chief, but I don't feel worthy of him. I realize I have Native American blood, but I still feel like a stranger here. I feel as if we Americans did him wrong. We did.

The trail from eastern Montana into Canada is rough and it is cold, but one night when I go to sleep with the Sioux, I wake transported. I wonder where. I'm wearing a gray Confederate army uniform like the one I saw in a museum. I'm dressed like a man. I see a Confederate flag and another flag waving in the breeze. It is green as grass with a yellow harp and angel symbol in the center. These are Confederate people, an Irish brigade. Where am I and why am I dressed like a man? I know how I got here. As Tituba explained to me, I'm dreaming. I'm not really dead and I'm not really here. I think of my DNA pie chart. Can this be part of the Irish slice of my pie.

"Okay, you Louisiana Tigers, get to that line," Major Chatham Wheat yells. With that, I know where I am. I recognize him from a picture when I studied the Irish Confederates.

"I'm in the American Civil War on the Confederate side," I whisper to no one in particular. "They lose the Civil War. So I go from being with Sitting Bull and winning against Custer to being in the American Civil War with these Irish Confederates and losing."

"I'm with an Irish brigade." I am in a hand-dug trench. I peer over the side of the trench and see a wagon full of injured men being drawn by a mule. I hear men moaning with pain or maybe hunger, but I think that they are injured because they are moaning loudly. Blood drips from the back of the wagon. My stomach turns a flip. Hearing their pain makes me feel squeamish. I may faint. I hate the sight of blood and the sounds of other people's pain. I try to control myself, but it doesn't work. It is almost dark, but flashes of gunfire light the night sky. If this wasn't a war, the flashes would look beautiful like fireworks.

This is 1862. I need to return to 2022. I needed for Tituba to tell me how before I left her, but I had left her abruptly. I haven't been able to figure it out on my own. I think back over the things she told me, but I still don't know. She said I would be sleeping and wake back home where I was supposed to be. She said I had a head injury that was causing my travels.

I'm certain I don't believe her.

Suddenly, the night becomes silent except for the moaning of some of the men. There is a full moon, and it looks as if all is well with the world. The sick and injured men are being hauled away. I wonder where the hospital is although I know that I can't work in it. I faint too easily.

Smelling the moist dirt, I peer over the edge of the trench again, and in the moonlight, I see several lone men sneak into the Union camp. I watch to see what happens. Then I hear men in normal conversation like they are in a bar enjoying themselves. I see the tips of cigars or cigarettes being lighted with matches. I realize how close this trench is to the Union camp for me to hear their conversations. These men fight by day and fraternize at night and share tobacco. I read that they often know each other or may even be brothers. This is an awful war. All wars are awful.

My stomach begins to growl. I remember Tiny Bird naming me Growl One. I miss Tiny Bird. I miss Aud. I miss Audrey. I wonder how Tiny Bird faired with the English invaders. Perhaps they didn't kill her. I hope not. At Salem, I never heard anything about it, but the timing and the year had been wrong.

A soldier in the trench near me says, "I would like to give you some food, but we ran out of rations days ago. All we have is some hard tack, wormy biscuits, and I wouldn't suggest that you eat them. Unless you are ready to die."

"Thanks for the warning."

"Well, blarney, you are a woman. What are you doing here?"

"I really don't know." I answer truthfully.

"Well, I'm sorry that we have no food. If we had some, I would share."

"Me too. But thank you," I reply, trying to think when I ate last. I touched my ribcage. I could feel bones. I look at the soldier who told me about the biscuits. He isn't wearing any shoes, and my uniform looks better than his. I remembered that the Confederates ran out of uniforms and materials to make more. The one that I'm wearing probably came off a dead man.

"Where did you get your boots?"

I am still wearing my shield maiden boots. How is that possible? They made it from the Vikings to the Powhatans to Little Bighorn to Salem and now here. I notice him looking at my boots.

I don't think he has ever seen anything like my boots before. "Native American?"

"No. I could tell you that they were bought for me in Vinland by a Viking man in 992, but you wouldn't believe me."

"Mame', you need something to eat. You are hallucinating."

"No, I'm really not. You are just dreaming. I'm not really here. Well, not according to Tituba."

"Tituba? What is that? A leprechaun? You believe in leprechauns?

"It is a who; not a what. She was tried as a witch at the Salem witch trials. For that matter, I was too."

The Irish soldier stared at me in disbelief. "You can try to sneak into the Union camp and steal some of their food."

"I watched some soldiers sneak in a few minutes ago for tobacco. They smoked it with the Union soldiers as if friends."

"Yeah. Some are friends. Some are even brothers. This is a crazy war. It is mostly a rich man's war and not really over slavery. I hear."

"I think that General Grant intercepts the messages between the Confederate generals, so he always knows what they are planning, thinking, and doing. I don't know why I'm here. I really need to leave."

"Where will you go?"

"I really need to get back to my daughter."

"How can I help?"

"I'm not sure that you can, but thank you. I needed to see a friendly face. I think I' will sleep now. Suddenly, I am very tired."

"Me, too, lady. We are all exhausted."

Chapter 16

I wake to lots of noisy people. It is Mardi Gras in New Orleans. Finally, it is 2022. I know because I see decorative blow-up balloons stating the year. I am staying in a room above the French Quarter. I don't know how I got here or why. The noisy crowd is having a grand time. I get out of bed and walk to the window and out on the balcony. Policemen are ushering the crowd back up the street on horseback. This is the last day. Mardi Gras is over. The policemen look exhausted. I've been here before during Mardi Gras. People try to do things here while inebriated during Mardi Gras in New Orleans that they wouldn't dare do anywhere else. They lose their inhibitions.

I look at my clothes. I'm still wearing gray Confederate soldier's pants and my shield maiden boots. My clothing is covered in dirt. Here what you are wearing isn't a problem unless you start flashing people. Brief flashes of breasts will slide with the police, but anything else is liable to get you arrested.

I look for my cell phone to text Audrey. It isn't on the side table, and I can't find my purse. It must have gotten lost when the *Titanic* sunk. On the *Titanic* is the last time I remember having it. My head is hurting, so I lie back on the bed to rest for a few minutes. Since the police are closing the Mardi Gras festivities, things should get quieter soon. Maybe I can go back to sleep and sleep off this terrible headache and fatigue.

I sleep fitfully, but wake to find that I'm naked. I hope that I'm not lying in the Confederate hospital with a lot of men or anywhere near the Mardi Gras festivities. I wonder if I can dream while dreaming. I glance around the room, trying to find a sheet or blanket to cover myself. Once I'm covered with a sheet, I look around at this hospital room. I'm in a room by myself. It is more modern looking than a field hospital from the American Civil War. I don't know where I am, but I don't think I'm still in the trenches of the American Civil War, and definitely I'm not in a trench with an Irish soldier. This may be what Tituba meant by I was only dreaming. She said that I would wake. I remember having dreams before that my teeth or hair had fallen out and waking to touch my mouth or head to make sure it was a dream, and I still had my hair and teeth.

A nurse comes into the room, "Ms. Monroe, you have a visitor."

"Wait, my name is Heidi Lodbrok. I thought you called me Monroe." I look for a hospital wrist identification bracelet. There isn't one.

The nurse looks at me and shakes her head. I'm not certain which of us is confused. "We had to pump your stomach, Ms. Monroe. Those barbiturates messed you up, but you will be okay now. You have visitors."

"Who?" I couldn't have any visitors if I am naked. "What year is this? Why am I taking barbiturates? Why are you calling me Ms. Monroe?" I wondered if my hearing was also distorted. My head still aches, and I'm still fatigued. I touch my scalp. There is a strip of about a hundred stitches running across the top of my head.

"1963." She didn't answer my other questions.

"Dang. I've been transported again, but not to 2022. I was in 2022 in the French Quarter in New Orleans. I went to sleep to get some rest. I wanted to stay there. I'm sure I could have made it to Memphis from there."

"What do you mean? Not 2022? This is February 9, 1964."

"I don't have on any clothes. I'm totally naked. Why? I can't have a visitor? I don't want any visitors until you bring me some clothes. I'm naked."

"You took off your own street clothes, gray woolen pants and a white shirt, Ms. Monroe. Your clothing was covered with dirt. We gave you a hospital gown. You said that clothes were restrictive, so you refused to put the hospital gown on."

"Well, I don't want a visitor I don't want to see people without my clothes. Please stop calling me Ms. Monroe and show me how to turn on the television. Where is the remote? I want to watch the Beatles. What time is it?"

The nurse had said February 9, 1964. I thought. This is the first day that the Beatles were on the Ed Sullivan Show. Apparently, she thinks that I'm Marilyn Monroe. No, that can't be right. Marilyn Monroe died August 4, 1962. I can't be Marilyn. I would already be dead. I remembered singing at President Kennedy's birthday celebration. I'm confused, or the nurse is confused. Maybe I'm Monroe's ghost, but ghosts don't need to get their stomachs pumped. Maybe I'm a Ghost Dancer from Sitting Bull's vision. Maybe the nurse had Marilyn Monroe in here a few years back. Maybe I look like her except I have a large scar.

There is no remote. The television has one on and off knob and only three channels that you turn to change by hand. The television show begins with a live audience in The Ed Sullivan Theater with some famous people in attendance like Richard Nixon's daughters. Sullivan tells the audience that Elvis Presley and his manager sent the Beatles a telegram. I know better than that. Elvis didn't even know about it. Entertainers are like politicians; they lie. Their first song, "All My Loving" is followed by "Till There was You." The names of the group members is superimposed on close-up shots. John Lennon's picture shows "SORRY GIRLS, HE'S MARRIED." Then they sing "She Loves You." After a prerecorded appearance by magician Fred Kaps, the Beatles return and sing "I Saw Her Standing There" and "I Want to Hold Your Hand."

I am smitten. I have always been a Beatles fan, but this is wonderful, although in black and white and in 1964. I am truly enjoying this although I feel like I've seen it before. Perhaps this is the English part of my ancestry DNA pie chart. Perhaps not.

Again, the nurse comes in the door and says, "You have a visitor, Mrs. Lodbrok."

Here are your street clothes." The last clothes I remember wearing were the Army uniform of the Confederate soldier. Those are what she is handing to me. "We have had the clothes cleaned. If you wish to see your visitors, put these on. Your visitors are still waiting. That man said he would wait forever."

"Man? Who is he?"

"He said his name is Rollo. Now, there is a young girl with him. She says that she is your daughter. Her boyfriend flew in from Colorado. They say that they can get married now that you are better."

"My daughter, Audrey?"

"Yes. She said her name is Audrey. She is a very beautiful young lady. She has been here every day. Rollo has too."

"But that can't be. Rollo is a Viking and Audrey is in 2022. How long have I been here in this hospital? I thought this was 1964."

"You've been here since you were brought back here after your car accident. They flew you to Memphis from England. You don't remember any of that do you? People with head injuries rarely remember much prior to the injury and especially on the day of the accident."

"My name is Heidi Lodbrok. You have been calling me Marilyn. I thought you had me mixed up with Marilyn Monroe."

"Oh, my goodness, no," the nurse answered. "Yes, Ms. Lodbrok. I know who you are. Do you? Can you tell me what your birthday is? You do remind me of her with the refusal to wear clothes, but she's been dead for two years. Didn't you know?"

I let the question pass. "You said my daughter was here. How can that be? She was born in 2000."

"I don't know about all that, but I don't see how that can be since she is waiting in the lobby for you to get dressed, so here, put these on. You do seem to still be disoriented. Can I help you?"

"No, I can do it. I can dress myself. It seems I'm not the only person who is disoriented. Do you know about Sitting Bull's vision?"

"What? Did you say something about Sitting Bull?"

"Oh, nothing," I answer.

I dress in the clean gray pants and the white shirt, sans a bra. She hadn't brought me one. I hope the white shirt isn't see through.

The nurse hadn't brought any underwear either like panties, so I just put on my outer clothes. The shoes were a funny looking sort. These are not my shield maiden clothes or shoes. They looked like black slip on shoes much like the Puritans wore. I slip on the clothes and shoes. I feel naked without any underwear and socks. How can the year be 1964? I think the nurse is mistaken about the year too since she was calling me Monroe. She thinks I'm disoriented. They say healthcare workers are stressed out because of the Covid 19 pandemic. Perhaps she is so stressed that she doesn't know the year. If it isn't her, it must be me.

Once dressed, I press the button for a nurse. Soon she opens the door and brings in a wheelchair. She helps me into it and she pushes me toward the lobby, but we stop before I go around the corner. I ask her to leave me here. She hesitates, but does as I ask. I peer around the corner at my visitors. There are three people that I see sitting there. I recognize Audrey, but there is a young man and an older man with Audrey. The young one must be her fiance`. Or maybe they have already gotten married, and I missed the wedding. I so wanted to be back in America with her, but I didn't know how to get back here. I remember Tituba, the woman who was tried for being a witch when I was in Salem, telling me that I hadn't really left that it was all a dream. I don't really believe that. If all this was a dream, how was she communicating with me? I wonder who the other man is. The nurse said him name was Rollo. This man was not Rollo the Viking.

Audrey and Matthew look so happy and so anxious at the same time. How do I explain to them that I've been traveling all-over the world? How does Audrey even know about Rollo? I look at the older man more closely. He doesn't even resemble Rollo the Viking in the least. I don't remember who this man is, but apparently, he knows who I am. The nurse said that Rollo was here. Maybe I don't have to explain. I roll my wheelchair around the corner.

"Hi," I say. They all three get out of their chairs at the same time. Audrey looks like she's seen a ghost, but hurries to hug me first. I think about Crazy Horse's vision of the Ghost Dancers.

"Ah, Mom, it is so good to see you up and around. I've been so worried about you," Audrey says. "We had you brought back to Memphis from England so we could be with you, but Covid 19 has made that difficult to get to visit.

I didn't know what to say, so I said, "Have I missed the wedding?"

"No, you haven't. We waited for you to regain consciousness. Now that you have, we can go on with our plans. If you feel up to it."

"Have I been here in this hospital the entire time?" Then without hearing her reply, I turn to the older gentleman. "Who are you?" I ask. "I thought the nurse said Rollo was here. Who are you, and where is Rollo the Viking?"

"I have been here all the time. Audrey and I sat beside your hospital bed for days on end. You just regained consciousness yesterday, but you are still a little disoriented. The nurse said you thought you were Marilyn Monroe," the man that isn't Rollo says.

"The nurse called me Ms. Monroe, but then I saw the Beatles on television. Marilyn Monroe died before the Beatles came to America. Speaking of coming to America, how did you get here?" I ask the man that isn't Rollo, who then looks at Audrey with an I don't know what to say look.

Then the man just continued to look at me, but he didn't answer.

I guess he is being polite.

So I turned to Audrey, "Please introduce your fiance'. I've been waiting to meet him."

Audrey looks at the young man and smiles broadly, "Mom, this is Matthew. We are getting married. I'm so sorry that I didn't go with you on your flight to England. Perhaps I would have been driving, and there wouldn't have been a wreck. I'm so sorry. You have been unconscious for such a long while, for many weeks."

"When is the wedding?" I couldn't think on anything else to say. Someday, I would tell her about all my adventures as a world walker, but today didn't seem like the time. She probably wouldn't believe me anyway.

"Whenever you are able to get out of the hospital, we will get married. Everything is planned. Well, everything except the date. We will talk more about it tomorrow. You still seem somewhat disoriented. Where did you get these clothes? Shoes? The shoes look like those worn during the first Thanksgiving." She looks at the gray wool pants and the linen shirt that I am wearing. Her face turns bright red. She is embarrassed for Matthew to see me wearing these clothes.

"I think they were," I reply. "The nurse brought them to me. I need to go back to my room. These bright lights are giving me a headache. I don't want anyone to tell me I'm disoriented again.

"Oh, Mom, I'm sorry," Audrey says. She pushes my wheelchair around the corner and back down the hall to my room. Suddenly, the nurse appears and helps me inside the room and back into my bed. This time, I change into her horrible hospital gown instead of remaining naked. This time she doesn't call me Ms. Monroe. Once alone again, I think about the clothes and shoes that I had been wearing. If all my travels were just a dream as Tituba had told me, why do I have these clothes and shoes?

I do not remember the man who calls himself Rollo. Could he be my husband John Lodbrok? I don't recognize him. I would like to see the real Rollo the Viking. John and I were separated before I left for England. I don't know why he is calling himself Rollo.

Days go by before I am dismissed from the hospital. While here, I lie awake and think of my world traveling adventures. I am having a very difficult time believing that I've been asleep and dreaming all these things. The travels have been real and the emotions too. I've been frightened. I've been happy. I've been sad, but through it all, I've missed Audrey. Some of my adventures have taught me things I didn't learn from a book or from research on the internet. I learned much about the *Titanic*, including Molly Brown and Captain Smith. I felt the chaos and danger after hitting the iceberg. I learned the unique tastes and smells of the Vikings food and honey mead. I learned to appreciate the craftsmanship of the Viking ship builders. I learned to appreciate the resourcefulness of the Powhatan women. I learned the superstitions of the Puritans during the Salem Witch Trials. I saw that the American Civil War was between friends and often brothers who shared conversations, tobacco, and food. I learned the vengeance of the Native Americans at Little Big Horn. I enjoyed the Beatles, but not Marilyn Monroe.

On the day I am discharged from the hospital, John brings me clothes much like the tourist uniform I wore to England and on the *Titanic-* jeans, tee, and sweatshirt. The man who calls himself Rollo checks me out of the hospital and takes me home with him. He is excited about giving Audrey away at her wedding, so I guess he is her father John Lodbrok. I still don't remember him. I don't plan to share a bedroom with him. I still miss Rollo the Viking.

When we arrive home, he knows the code to my house to my house alarm. He helps me inside. He is very helpful, making me comfortable and getting me something to eat. I look around the den. There aren't any pictures of us as a family. I find that disturbing. I thought there would be pictures of us as a family if he was John Lodbrok who calls himself Rollo. I go to my bedroom. I guess it is his bedroom too. I open the closet door in our bedroom. His clothes are hanging on one side of the closet. I see a black tux in a plastic bag hanging there on the right. I am still confused. I see that I have two new dresses in plastic bags hanging in my side of the closet. One is navy and one is pink. I realize that Audrey bought me these for the wedding. They look similar in style. Audrey would want me to look like her mother, not her sister.

I get clean pajamas from the top drawer of a chest of drawers in the corner of the room. The clothes in this drawer smell like lavendar. I look at these pajamas. They are flannel with small printed pink roses. I don't remember ever wearing them. I head to the bathroom to take a hot, soaking bath. I don't think I've soaked in a tub of hot water since I flew to England. I lock the bathroom door and step into the glorious hot water. I remember locking the bathroom door in Captain Smith's quarters on the *Titanic*.

The warmth of the water feels so good to my tired body. I think about the dinner with Captain Smith on the *Titanic*. I remember the smell of the French gardenia shampoo. I love that smell. I always will, although I didn't care for Captain Smith. He was too condescending to me as a woman. American woman, he called me.

Tomorrow night is the wedding rehearsal and dinner at the Family Life Center at the church, and the next day is Audrey's wedding. I am glad I don't have to wear a dress like Mrs. Molly Brown gave me that belonged to her daughter. I guess the less formal pink dress is for the wedding rehearsal. I am so excited for her. After all my adventures, I finally made it home to Audrey in 2022 just in time for her to get married and move to Colorado. She wanted this so much. I wonder if Margaret Brown made it back home in time to see her grandson. There are many things I want to research: survivors of the *Titanic*, the Vikings, the Powhatans, the Salem witch trials, Custer's Last Stand, Sitting Bull, Marilyn Monroe and President Kennedy, the Irish Confederacy, French in New Orleans, the evidence of Vikings having come to America, and how an ancestry DNA test works and what to do if you think they made an error.

Audrey has already bought me everything that I'm to wear to the rehearsal dinner and to the wedding, so all I need do is get dressed and show up. She did that for me while I was in the hospital. No one has told me how long that I was in the hospital, and I have not told anyone about my world traveling adventures. They wouldn't believe me. I remember Tituba telling me that I was asleep and that I would wake up. Am I awake now? I have no way to prove these adventures. I feel like I may be crazy now. I don't tell anyone how crazy I feel. I must find something that proves that I traveled over the world. I don't remember who the man calls himself Rollo is. Apparently, he must be my husband John Lodbrok, but why don't I have pictures of him in my house?

John couldn't be more polite to me. He doesn't force anything. He talks about Audrey and her fiance'. He never mentions my accident or our break up.

Buying the wedding clothes and taking care of me in the hospital is Audrey's way of being certain that I would get well and get to go to her wedding, but my problems aren't just physical problems caused by the wreck. I remember my world adventures vividly, but I don't remember John. I try to remember him. Vaguely, I remember things that happened when Audrey was a small child that include John. What I remember about John is that we were separated for a few years before the ancestry DNA test. I can't remember why. I don't remember whether it was his fault or mine. I don't remember his coming back. As soon as, Audrey and Matthew leave for their honeymoon, I am going on a short vacation to Minnesota to find evidence of the Vikings and maybe the runic stone that that farmer found in his field. I'm desperate to find proof that the real Rollo visited America. I don't know what I'm looking to find. He was only on American soil with me for a few minutes before he was rescued by Leif Erickson's boat. He definitely shouldn't have a day named after him like Leif Erickson. Perhaps this time, I will find his sword or shield. I don't want the proof for anyone except myself, so I'm not going to explain any of this to John. He wouldn't understand. No one would. I don't understand it myself. I guess I should add interpreting dreams and dreaming while unconscious to my research.

I finish my bath only because the water has gotten cold, and I go out to the den in my pink rose printed pajamas. John looks at me and smiles. He is watching a football game. I sit on the couch. This feels like a typical situation to me. I take my lap top off the coffee table, open it, log into a travel website, and book a stay in a bed and breakfast with a Viking theme.

"Why do you want to go on a vacation there?" he asks as I show John the reservation to see his reaction. The vacation is for immediately after the wedding.

"I will go with you if you want me to. Are you certain that you feel up to traveling? When do you have to see the doctor again?"

"Yes. We will fly to Minnesota the afternoon after the wedding," I tell John. I will let him go with me on this trip if he wishes, but I'm not explaining my world traveling adventures to him or to anyone. Tituba said that I was dreaming and would wake. I am awake, but I still remember my adventures vividly.

Chapter 17

Finally, it is the day of Audrey and Matthew's wedding. John and I go to the church. I sneak into the bride's dressing room to see Audrey. Audrey looks beautiful in her dreamy cream-beige wedding gown with a long train with tiny pearls hand sewn on the vintage lace. On a closer look, I notice that the vintage parts of it that I recognize, especially the train. It reminds me of my own wedding gown. I think this is the train from my first wedding dress, the dress I wore when I married John Lodbrok.

I hug Audrey close, being careful not to ruin her hair and make up. "I love you, Audrey," I say. "I tried my best to return to you, and I made it. It was difficult." I smell her perfume. It smells of a rich mix of roses and gardenias.

Then I remember the suede feel and smoky smell of the leather Viking wedding dress that Rollo bought me. I remember that it was laced up the back as a one size fits most style and that Rollo himself helped me into the dress and laced it up snuggly. Although I was superstitious about him seeing me before the wedding, but it didn't fit as snuggly as that navy silk dress that had belonged to her daughter that Mrs. Molly Brown gave me to wear on the *Titanic*. I don't understand how these memories can be so strong.

A leather wedding dress would be too hot to wear in this sweltering and humid Memphis weather. The church is beautifully decorated with live flower arrangements of roses, gardenias in pots, and ferns. I feel sad that I was not available to help Audrey with these tremendous wedding preparations. There are beautiful floral arrangements with more roses hanging on the back of the pews and sitting on the window ledges in front of the immense stained glass windows. Each empty corner has a large fern. There are blooming gardenias sitting near the ferns. Flowers thrive in the Tennessee humidity, but the heat causes them to look thirsty and their petals to droop slightly. I feel slightly droopy myself. I think the excitement of Audrey's wedding has given me a shot of adrenaline, but I know that the energy will end whenever the day does or before. Otherwise, I don't think that I could make it. My strength hasn't fully returned since my stint in the hospital. I do not admit my fatigue to anyone, and I try to hide it in my movements and posture.

I think of the shield maiden outfit that Rollo bought for me and helped me into after our wedding. I loved those leather pants and vest. I especially loved the shield maiden boots Rollo bought me. Somehow my boots were traded for those ugly Puritan shoes that I wore with my Confederate soldiers gray woolen pants in the hospital. I don't know where I got either of those. Ironically, no one mentioned the contrast in time in my clothing with the Puritan shoes and the American Civil War pants.

Again, while I wait for Audrey, I think about my wedding to Rollo the Viking. I don't remember wondering about flowers the day that Rollo and I got married. I don't remember seeing flowers in Vinland or Finland. I was thinking of the trip to America on his Viking ship. I was thinking about getting back to Audrey. I remember being happy. I remember us hurrying to catch the tide.

I remember Ubba and Naddod. I remember Floke and Geishala. Were they from my dreams? Were they in my dreams because I had taught about the Vikings in my history classroom or watched The Vikings on television.

Then I think of teaching the Powhatan women to make shield maiden clothes. I wonder what happened to Aud and Tiny Bird. I think of Rollo and me saving Aud as a changeling.

I am escorted down the aisle to my designated pew near the front of the church. The organist begins playing the wedding march. We stand to honor Audrey, the bride. John escorts Audrey down the aisle and gives her away. She looks beautiful. Then he comes to sit beside me. In my mind, I compare Audrey's wedding to my own wedding to Rollo. My wedding to Rollo wasn't consummated, so I guess it wasn't a true wedding. I guess I was still married to John Lodbrok. Being married to two men at the same time is against the law. What was I thinking? I try to remember my wedding to John, but those memories are gone, but John is still here. My steadfast husband the father of Aud. My head injury at the car accident wiped out many of my memories of him. I wonder if those memories will return.

Finally after vows and special music, the pastor announces that all guests are invited to a reception in the Family Life Center. Audrey and Matthew welcome and greet their guests. John and I stand in the line, too. I get so tired that I can not think. John notices my discomfort and gets me a chair. Finally, Audrey and Matthew leave for their honeymoon. I have enough energy to hug her good-bye. Then John takes me home.

All the way home, I wonder if I will be able to go on the trip that I've planned to Minnesota. I undress and put on my pajamas with the pink roses. I go into the bathroom to remove my make up and brush my teeth. I think of his caring for me since I've gotten out of the hospital. While I'm standing there with the toothbrush in my mouth, John knocks on the bathroom door. "While you were in the hospital, this package came for you," he says and hands it to me. "It is probably something that you ordered from Amazon."

Of course, I don't remember ordering anything, so I say, "Put it in there on the bed. I'll open it when I get there."

I finish my nightly routine and head to bed. I look at the package. It isn't from Amazon. It has a return address of somewhere in Maine. I open the box. It is the White Star Line ale bottle with my ancestry DNA results inside, the ale bottle that I tossed off the side of the *Titanic*. I have my proof.

I cancel our trip to Minnesota. That Rollo is long gone. but this one is still here as steadfast as ever.

The End